MEET THE FORTUNES!

Fortune of the Month: Oliver Fortune Hayes

Age: 37

Vital statistics: Blue-eyed, exceedingly handsome aristocrat and single dad. He's just a tad...uptight.

Claim to Fame: Sir Oliver is rich. *Really* rich.

Romantic prospects: Suddenly he's got a toddler in diapers and a dog barely housebroken. Just how much are most women willing to take on?

"I can manage millions, but when it comes to my small Fortune, I haven't a clue. Shannon makes it all look so easy. She can handle baby Ollie and even get barking Barnaby to toe the line. But when Shannon and I are together, I feel as though I'm losing control all over again. She's too young for me, too exuberant, too...Shannon. The logical part of me says I should hightail it back to London before anyone gets hurt. But there's another part that says, *What if*..."

THE FORTUNES OF TEXAS:
COWBOY COUNTRY:
Lassoing hearts from across the pond!

Dear Reader,

This book was such a pleasure to write because it allowed me to revisit the Fortune family (whom I dearly love) in Horseback Hollow. A special treat was to be able to have two of my characters from last year (Jude Fortune and Gabi Mendoza in *A Sweetheart for Jude Fortune*) marry in this book, along with three of Jude's other siblings.

While I couldn't imagine sharing my wedding day with siblings, I believe if I could have done it Fortune style, it would have been worth it.

This book has everything: kids, dogs, all the Fortunes and lots of new and exciting things going on in Horseback Hollow!

By the way, this is also the first book that I did a Pinterest board on. I'd love for you to check it out. The name of the board is "Fortune's Little Heartbreaker."

Also, if you're so inclined, like me on Facebook and follow @cindykirkauthor on Twitter. I'd love for us to stay connected.

Warmest regards,

Cindy Kirk

Fortune's Little Heartbreaker

—

Cindy Kirk

HARLEQUIN® SPECIAL EDITION®

Special thanks and acknowledgment to Cindy Kirk for her contribution to the Fortunes of Texas: Cowboy Country continuity.

ISBN-13: 978-0-373-65865-7

Fortune's Little Heartbreaker

Copyright © 2015 by Harlequin Books S.A.

Recycling programs for this product may not exist in your area.

Printed in U.S.A.

HARLEQUIN®
www.Harlequin.com

From the time she was a little girl, **Cindy Kirk** thought everyone made up different endings to books, movies and television shows. Instead of counting sheep at night, she made up stories. She's now had over forty novels published. She enjoys writing emotionally satisfying stories with a little faith and humor tossed in. She encourages readers to connect with her on Facebook and Twitter @cindykirkauthor and via her website, cindykirk.com.

Books by Cindy Kirk

Harlequin Special Edition

Rx for Love

The Husband List
One Night with the Doctor
A Jackson Hole Homecoming
The Doctor and Mrs. Right
His Valentine Bride
The Doctor's Not-So-Little Secret
Jackson Hole Valentine
If the Ring Fits
The Christmas Proposition
In Love with John Doe
The Doctor's Baby

The Fortunes of Texas: Welcome to Horseback Hollow

A Sweetheart for Jude Fortune

The Fortunes of Texas: Southern Invasion

Expecting Fortune's Heir

Visit the Author Profile page at Harlequin.com for more titles.

This book is dedicated to some of my favorite Facebook friends and Fortunes of Texas fans:

Pamela Lowery

Deanna Vrba

Theresa Krupicka

Caro Carson

Nancy Greenfield

Veronica Mower

Mary Spicher

Dyan Carness

Brenda Schultes Bengard

Nancy Callahan Greenfield

Jennifer Faye

Sherri Shackelford

Ann Roth

Holmes Campbell

Michelle Major

Cheri Allan

Susan Meier

Betsy Ehrhardt

Kim Thomas

Laurie Brown

Deborah Farrand

Linda Conrad

Amanda Macfarlane

Lee Ann Kopp-Lopez

Chapter One

Shannon Singleton took a sip of the Superette's medium roast coffee and exhaled a happy sigh. Since returning to Horseback Hollow several months earlier, she'd come to realize how much she'd missed the town in north Texas where she'd grown up.

The postage-stamp eating area of the Superette consisted of three orange vinyl booths and two tables, each adorned with a bud vase of silk flowers. Nice, but no comparison to the cute little coffee shop Shannon used to frequent when she lived in Lubbock.

Still, the location was bright and cheery. Thanks to a wall of glass windows, Shannon even had a stellar view of the large pothole in the middle of the street.

"I wish they'd choose one of us and get it over with." Rachel Robinson expelled a frustrated sigh and sat back in the booth.

Shannon enjoyed meeting her friend every Tuesday

morning for coffee, but frankly was tired of obsessing over—and discussing—the job they both wanted.

It was a bit awkward, being in competition—again—with her friend. The other times Rachel had bested her, it had been over inconsequential things; like the last piece of dessert at the Hollows Cantina or the pair of boots they'd both spotted at that cute little boutique in Vicker's Corners.

This time was different. *This* time the outcome mattered. Professional positions in this small town an hour south of Lubbock were few and far between. And Shannon really wanted the marketing job with the Fortune Foundation.

In the four years since graduation from Texas Tech with a degree in business, all of Shannon's experience had been in marketing. Rachel had readily admitted she didn't have experience in the marketing arena.

But that fact didn't mean squat. Just as with those pretty turquoise boots, it seemed whenever she and Rachel competed for anything, Rachel came out ahead.

"Earth to Shannon."

Shannon brought the cup to her lips and focused on her friend. She and Rachel were both in their midtwenties, had brown hair and similar interests. But that's where the comparison ended. Shannon considered herself slightly above average while Rachel was stunning. "What? Rewind."

"Wouldn't it be cool if they hired us both?" Rachel smiled at the thought and broke off a piece of scone. The woman's cheerful nature was just one of her many admirable qualities.

"I guess we'll find out…but not until the end of February." Shannon added more cream to her coffee, her tone pensive. "I don't see why it has to take that long. They completed interviews last month."

"It's probably because they're just getting this office

location up and running," Rachel said, sounding way too understanding.

Of course her friend could afford to be charitable. She had a job and was earning her way. Shannon was back living with her parents and, other than the chores she performed at the ranch for her mom and dad, had been out of work for over two months. "Just between you and me, I can't believe they're going to open a foundation branch in Horseback Hollow."

"Doesn't surprise me." Rachel laughed. "This town is turning into a Fortune family hot spot."

The Fortunes were a wealthy family with business ventures all over the world. Their largest Texas base of operations was in Red Rock, just outside San Antonio. But there were also Fortunes in Horseback Hollow. Christopher Fortune Jones, who'd grown up in the area, would be heading the foundation branch in town.

"I'm tired of worrying about a job I might not get." To soothe her rising stress level, Shannon bit into the scone. *Oh, yeah, baby—sugar and blueberries, topped with a lemon glaze.* Talk about stress eating. She could almost feel her waistline expand.

"Are you going to the party on Saturday?" Rachel asked, changing the subject.

The "party" was actually a couple's baby shower being thrown by friends. The fact it was a couple's baby shower practically guaranteed there wouldn't be any unattached men attending. After all, what single straight guy would willingly give up his Saturday night to attend such an event?

"I promised Gabi I'd attend." Shannon paused and narrowed her gaze. Outside, a sleek black car she didn't recognize pulled into the lot. "My other choice is playing cards with my parents and their friends."

Rachel gave an exaggerated shudder.

"It's not that bad." Shannon liked her parents and enjoyed the members of their card club. In fact, if she hadn't given Gabi Mendoza her word she'd show, she'd be seriously tempted to skip the shower and play cards instead.

Rachel took a sip of her chai tea. "I'm crossing my fingers there'll be some fresh meat at this little soiree."

"Don't hold your breath." Shannon could have said more but pressed her lips shut. Let the woman have her dreams…

Rachel startled her by emitting a low whistle and pointing to the window. "Get a load of that."

"I saw it." Obligingly, Shannon leaned forward for a better look. Just south of the humongous pothole sat a shiny vehicle that cost more than she used to make in a year. It was rare to see such an expensive car in Horseback Hollow. "Mercedes."

"Forget the car." Though they were alone in the café, Rachel's voice was soft, almost reverent. "Feast your eyes on him."

Shannon swung her gaze from the sleek lines and shiny black finish of the SL250 to focus on the tall, broad-shouldered man with dark brown hair exiting the vehicle.

A man obviously on a mission, he rounded the back of the car with decisive steps. When he bent over to retrieve something from the backseat, Shannon's lips curved.

"Ooh la la," Rachel breathed.

For a second Shannon forgot how to breathe as the pristine white shirt stretched tight across the breadth of shoulders, muscular legs encased in dark trousers.

Shannon's heart quivered. "If his face is half as good as his backside, we're in for a treat."

As if in answer to her prayer, the guy straightened and turned. Ooh la la, indeed. He had classically handsome features with a strong jaw, straight nose and cheekbones that looked as if they had been chiseled from granite. She'd wager his stylishly cut dark hair had never seen the insides of a Cut 'N' Curl.

Yes, indeed, the man was an impressive hunk of masculinity even with sunglasses covering his eyes.

While the set of those shoulders and confident stance said "don't mess with me," messing with him was just what Shannon longed to do. Until she saw two little legs dangling from the blanketed bundle he'd pulled from the car.

Rachel expelled a heavy sigh, apparently seeing the evidence of daddy-hood, as well. "He's got a kid."

Her friend sounded as disappointed as Shannon felt.

"Figures he'd be taken." Shannon heaved her own sigh. "The cute ones always are."

"Marriage doesn't stop some of them from sniffing around."

"My old boss Jerry was a perfect example of that." Even as she spoke, Shannon's gaze returned to the dark-haired stranger.

"You taught Jerry the Jerk not to mess with you."

Shannon just smiled and shrugged. Lately she'd begun to wonder if there was a way she could have handled the situation differently and kept her job.

Water under a collapsed bridge.

The man shut the door firmly, then stepped away, giving Shannon a glimpse of a furry head with perked-up ears, little paws braced on the dash. She couldn't stop a smile. She loved animals almost as much as she loved children. "He's got a dog, too."

Rachel looked up from the text she'd glanced down to read. Apparently discovering the stranger had a kid had turned her initial interest to indifference.

"The hot guy has a kid *and* a dog," Shannon told her friend.

"Bet you five he also has a wife with blond hair and a killer figure." Rachel's tone turned philosophical. "That's practically a given with guys like him."

Shannon grinned. "Aren't you the cynical one?"

"Realist." Rachel popped a bite of scone into her mouth. "I should have known he was too good to be single."

Shannon rolled her eyes.

"He's coming inside," Rachel hissed.

Shannon turned in her chair just as the automatic doors of the Superette slid open.

Francine, the store's lone cashier, was in the back of the store stocking shelves. Since they were the only customers, Frannie had told them to holler if someone showed and was ready to check out.

The man paused just inside the entrance and removed his sunglasses. He glanced at the empty checkout counter, impatience wrapped around him like a too-tight jacket. Shannon expected any second he'd start tapping his foot.

Shannon pulled to her feet and crossed to him, wishing she was wearing something—anything—besides jeans and a faded Texas Tech T-shirt. "May I help you?"

The man was silent for a second, staring at her. His eyes were a cool blue with a darker rim. Shannon forced herself to hold that piercing gaze.

"I find myself in need of some assistance," he said after a couple of seconds, his smile surprisingly warm and charming. "My GPS has gone bonkers. I'm looking for a ranch called the Broken R."

In addition to the killer smile, the man had a totally de-lish British accent. Shannon surreptitiously slanted a glance down but his ring finger was hidden beneath the blankets.

"Are you a relative?" Though Shannon didn't like to

pry, Rachel would kill her if she didn't get at least one or two deets.

"I'm Jensen's brother." He adjusted his stance as the child beneath the blanket stirred. "Are you familiar with the location?"

Shannon couldn't tell if the toddler was a boy or girl. The shoes were gray leather sneakers that could belong to either sex. The only thing she could see above the blanket was a thatch of slightly wavy brown hair.

"It's super easy to find." Shannon quickly gave him directions. She offered to write them down, but he told her there was no need.

"Thank you." He smiled again and his whole face relaxed. "You've been very kind."

Though she wanted to volunteer to ride with him and show him the way, Shannon resisted the temptation. Married men were not on her radar.

Still, she remained where she was and watched him stroll to the car. Once he reached the vehicle, she scurried over to where Rachel waited.

"Ohmigod." Rachel's eyes sparkled. "His accent is incredible."

"The rest of him is pretty incredible too." Shannon surreptitiously watched Jensen Fortune Chesterfield's hot brother buckle the child into the seat. The blanket around the toddler fell to the concrete but was quickly scooped up.

"He's definitely a boy," she told her friend.

"You're wrong." Rachel chuckled. "That one is all man."

"Not him. The kid. I couldn't tell initially boy or girl, but he's wearing a Thomas the Tank Engine shirt. Definitely a boy."

"Who cares about the child?" Rachel fluttered her long lashes. "Did you hear that fantabulous British accent?"

"You said that before."

"It bears repeating."

The sleek black sedan backed up and headed out of the lot, careful to avoid the asphalt crater.

"It doesn't matter." Shannon sighed and turned her attention back to her scone. "Like you said, a guy that gorgeous has a beautiful wife somewhere."

Oliver Fortune Hayes once had a beautiful wife. Then he'd had a beautiful ex-wife. Now, the stunningly beautiful blonde was gone.

"Diane was killed in a car accident two months ago," Oliver told his brother Jensen. He kept his tone matter-of-fact, tamping down any emotion. "She was in the car with a man she'd been seeing for quite some time. He also died in the crash."

The two men sat in Jensen's kitchen, having a cup of tea. Thanks to the concise directions from the pretty brunette at the grocery shop, Oliver had easily found the Broken R ranch. Jensen had been surprised to see him a full twenty-four hours earlier than expected and apologetic that Amber was in Lubbock shopping.

Oliver looked forward to meeting his brother's fiancée but appreciated the opportunity to talk privately first.

Jensen hadn't changed much since Oliver had last seen him. His brother's dark hair was perhaps a trifle longer but he was still the very proper British gentleman that Oliver remembered. Though the cowboy boots were a shock, Jensen's gray trousers were perfectly creased, and his white dress shirt startlingly white.

"This is the first I've heard of Diane's death. Why didn't you call?" Jensen was his half brother from the second marriage of Oliver's mother. Though seven years separated them in age, Oliver had always been fond of Jensen. When Oliver had announced his intention to come to

Horseback Hollow after their sister, Amelia, gave birth, Jensen had offered to let him stay at his ranch.

"My life has been topsy-turvy since the moment I found out." He'd discovered Diane had died at a cocktail party when a mutual friend had expressed sympathy.

"I bet."

Oliver continued as if Jensen hadn't spoken. "Diane's parents didn't notify me. They took Ollie into their home even though they knew full custody immediately reverted to me upon her death. They kept my son from me."

Jensen flinched at the underlying anger in his brother's carefully controlled tone. "I'm surprised they didn't put up a fight once you found out and arrived on their door-step to claim him."

"There would have been no point." Oliver waved a hand. "I'm the child's father."

"Given your lifestyle, taking on a child had to be dif-ficult."

"Once I established a schedule, it went quite well," Oli-ver said in a clipped tone, irritated his brother could think him incapable of caring for one small boy. "The nanny I hired is excellent and believes as strongly as I do in the importance of a routine. And she fully understood why I needed to make this trip. Unfortunately she refuses to leave the country."

Jensen obviously had nothing to add. He didn't have children. Not even a wife. Not yet anyway.

Oliver glanced down, noting Barnaby had fallen asleep at his feet. He only hoped his son was sleeping as soundly as the dog. The moment he'd arrived at the ranch, Oliver had put Ollie down for a nap. After a sixteen-hour flight from London to Lubbock the day before, even the brief respite in a hotel overnight hadn't been enough sleep for a toddler.

His son had been fussy after the long flight and had kept Oliver up most of the night. Oliver had dreaded the forty-five-minute car ride from Lubbock to Horseback Hollow, but the child had fallen asleep while Oliver was strapping him into his car seat. He'd slept during the entire trip, not waking even when Oliver brought him inside and laid him on Jensen's bed.

Jensen's gaze dropped to the corgi. "What's his name?"

"Barnaby." Oliver wasn't sure who was more surprised at the fondness in his voice, him or his brother.

"You don't like dogs."

"I've never disliked them," Oliver corrected. "I simply never had time for one. Diane purchased Barnaby for Ollie when she left me. He's quite attached to the animal."

"You're going to keep him?"

"Are you referring to Ollie? Or Barnaby?"

"Both." Jensen grinned. "I've never considered you the kid or dog type."

"Ollie is my son. My responsibility. When Diane and I split up, I thought our child's needs would be better served living with her. That's the only reason I didn't fight for custody. I've already explained about the dog."

Jensen stared contemplatively at the animal that had awakened and now sat, brown eyes scanning the room, ears perked up like two radio antennae.

"Corgis are herding animals."

Oliver nodded. "I observed some of that behavior when he first came to live with me. But that's no longer an issue."

"You have the dog on a schedule, too."

"Certainly."

"Is Barnaby a dog that goes in and out?" Jensen asked in a tone that was a little too casual.

Oliver cocked his head.

"Could he be an outside dog?"

Oliver thought for a moment, considered. "He likes being outdoors, but I don't believe he's suited to roughing it."

Jensen rubbed his chin. "That presents a problem."

"How so?"

"Amber is allergic to dogs." His brother grimaced. "Come to think of it, I probably shouldn't have let the animal in the house."

Ah, now Oliver understood. "No worries. I'll stay with Mother."

"You're forgetting something, aren't you?"

"Am I?"

"Mother is also allergic." Jensen's expression was solemn. "Remember the puppy Father brought home? She got congested and broke out in hives."

Bugger. He'd forgotten all about that episode. He'd been older and away at boarding school, so the fact that the dog had to be returned to the breeder hadn't affected him.

"It appears I'll have to rent a suite at a hotel." Oliver gave a shrug. "Is there one you'd recommend?"

Jensen gave a hoot of laughter. "You saw the extent of our business district when you stopped at the Superette."

Was his brother teasing him? The way he used to when he was a bit of a boy? "I assumed the more populated area of the city was elsewhere."

"Horseback Hollow isn't a city, it's a town. There are no hotels, motels or even any B and Bs." Jensen's expression sobered. "Right now there isn't even a hotel in Vicker's Corners. You'll have to go all the way to Lubbock to find one."

Oliver pressed his lips together. There was no way he'd flown across an entire ocean and half a continent to stay an hour away. Especially not with a child. The whole purpose of this trip was to spend time with family.

"There has to be a vacant house in the area," he told his brother. "Do you have the name of a real estate broker I could contact?"

"Now?"

"Since Ollie and I don't have accommodations for this evening, time is of the essence."

His brother rose and went to a desk where he pulled out a thin phone book. "I suggest starting with Shep Singleton. He's a local rancher and I believe he has an empty house on his property. I'm not sure if it would be satisfactory or what he'll want for rent—"

"Money won't be an issue if the house is clean and nearby."

"It's in a great location." Jensen pulled his brows together as if picturing the place in his mind. "It may even have a fenced yard."

"Do you have Mr. Singleton's mobile number?" Oliver pulled the phone from his jacket, his fingers poised above the keypad. He wanted to inspect this home. One way or the other, he would secure appropriate lodging for him and his son, today.

Because Oliver Fortune Hayes was used to going after—and getting—what he wanted.

Chapter Two

Shannon swore under her breath. She and Rachel had plans to see a movie in Lubbock this evening, then check out a Mexican place that had recently opened in the Depot District. Instead she'd had to call her friend and cancel.

All because her father had gotten a call from someone interested in renting the empty ranch house on the property. Apparently that someone had to see it immediately. There was no telling how long this would take. Or who the impatient person would turn out to be.

Her father only had a name...Oliver. He wasn't certain if that was the man's first or last name, as he'd been distracted during the call. One of his prize mares was foaling.

Shep Singleton might be focused on Sweet Betsy but Shannon was still his little girl. He ordered her to take one of the ranch hands with her for safety. It made sense, but she hated to pry them away from their duties.

The odds of Mr. Oliver being a serial killer or crazed

lunatic were next to nil. Besides, she'd had self-defense training and could hold her own.

When she pulled up in front of the home and saw a dusty Mercedes, a prickle of heat traveled up her spine. Surely it couldn't be…

Even as she hopped out of her dad's rusty pickup with the gash in the front end, the man from the Superette stepped from the vehicle. Ooh la la, he looked just as good as he had several hours ago and ready for business in his hand-tailored navy suit.

Smiling, Shannon crossed the gravel drive and extended her hand. "You must be Mr. Oliver?"

"Oliver Fortune Hayes," he corrected, smiling slightly. "And you're the helpful lady from the grocer's."

"Shannon Singleton." She gave his hand a decisive shake. "Shep's daughter. My dad said you wanted to check out the house."

"Indeed." Those amazing blue eyes settled on her, warm and friendly. "I appreciate you showing it on such short notice."

What was left of her irritation vanished. "Happy to do it."

He surprised her by turning back to the car. When he opened the back door and unfastened the boy from his car seat, she realized he hadn't come alone. Once the child's feet were firmly planted on the ground, the toddler looked around, gave an ear-splitting shriek and barreled after the corgi that had just leaped from the vehicle.

"That's Ollie. My son," Oliver told her, pride in his voice.

Oliver let the boy scamper a few yards before scooping him up. Ollie giggled and squirmed but settled when Oliver said something in a low tone.

"Barnaby."

The crisp sound of his name had the corgi turning. Oliver motioned with his hand and the dog moved to his side.

He looked, Shannon thought, like a man totally in control of the situation.

Oliver gazed speculatively at the house. "Since your father knows I'm looking for immediate occupancy, I assume the home is empty."

Shannon smiled. "You assume correctly."

The entire tour of the furnished home took all of five minutes. If Shannon hadn't been looking she might have missed the slight widening of Oliver's eyes when he first stepped inside the three-bedroom, thirteen-hundred-square-foot ranch house Shannon's grandparents had once called home.

Once she'd finished the tour, she rocked back on her boot heels, feeling oddly breathless. "What do you think?"

"I'll take it." Oliver put the boy down, reached into his back pocket and pulled out a wallet. "Sixty days with an option. I'll pay in advance."

"Just like that?" Decisiveness was one thing, but he hadn't asked a single question. "Don't you have any questions?"

"You've explained everything to my satisfaction." He kept one eye on his son, who was hopping like a frog across the living room. "The fact is, I need to secure lodging close to my family."

As Shannon opened her mouth, she wondered if she might be stepping over some line. But surely the man had other options. From what she'd observed of the Fortunes, they were a tight-knit family. "You're not staying with them?"

"That was the plan. But apparently Amber—my brother's

fiancée—is highly allergic to dogs. As is my mother, which I'd very inconveniently forgotten." He gestured with his head toward the corgi, who intently watched the hopping boy. "Ollie is very attached to Barnaby."

"He's a cutie. The boy, I mean. The dog is cute, too." Shannon paused to clear the babble from her throat before continuing. "Will your wife be joining you?"

For just an instant a spark of some emotion flickered in his eyes before the shutter dropped.

"Ollie's mother and I were divorced." His tone was matter-of-fact. "Well, Ms. Singleton?"

"Please call me Shannon."

"Well, *Shannon*. Do we have a deal?" He extended his hand.

When her fingers closed over his and a hot, unfamiliar riff of sensation traveled up her spine, something told Shannon that this deal might be more than she bargained for.

To Oliver's way of thinking, money smoothed most rough patches and made life extremely manageable. Unfortunately, in the past few days he hadn't found that to be as true as in the past. There hadn't been anyone to carry in his bags or help him unpack once he'd closed the deal on the ranch house.

Oliver glanced around the small living room, smiling at the sight of Ollie playing with his A-B-C bricks, the dog supervising from his position under the kitchen table. The place was so small he could see the kitchen from where he stood. Unbelievably, there was only one lavatory in the entire structure.

Since it was just him and Ollie, even when they added a nanny, it would be workable. Not ideal, but they would make do, much the way he had on those school camping trips when he'd been a boy. He decided to view the next two months as an adventure.

Both Ollie and Barnaby seemed to like the small space. Even Oliver had to admit he found his temporary residence comfortable, quiet and surprisingly homey. Still, after two days of settling in, he was ready to get to work. For that to happen, he needed a nanny.

He'd made inquiries, as had various family members. So far, none of the women he'd interviewed had been acceptable. Oliver would also consider a manny, but when he'd mentioned that to the woman at the agency in Lubbock, her eyebrows had shot up. She informed him mannies were scarcer in Texas than rain in August.

Man or woman, Oliver didn't care. He simply needed someone he could trust to tend to his son while he worked. He ran a busy brokerage firm in London. While he trusted and valued his employees, he prided himself on being personally involved with many of the firm's larger clients.

Dealing with time zone issues was frustrating enough, but then to have Ollie call to him or start crying over his bricks tumbling down was totally unacceptable. There had to be someone suitable in the area.

His hopes of finding someone from Horseback Hollow were rapidly fading. Amber had given him a couple of names, neither of whom was willing to live in. What good would they be to him living a half hour away? With the time differences an issue, if he needed to go out or simply make a phone call, he didn't want to wait.

The head of the placement agency guaranteed she'd find the perfect person, but kept asking him to give her more time. Well, he'd given her over two days. Since she couldn't make it happen, he would take the reins.

He pulled out his wallet and removed the card Miss

Shannon Singleton had given him to use in case of emergencies.

Oliver paused, considered. As far as he was concerned, being without a nanny for forty-eight hours qualified as an emergency.

Shannon stared at the phone in her hand for a second before dropping it into her bag.

Rachel slanted a questioning glance at her as they exited the movie theater in Vicker's Corners. "Who was that?"

"Oliver Fortune Hayes."

Shannon had told her friend all about playing rental agent with Mr. Fortune Hayes. Rachel had only one question— was he married?

"Mr. Hottie from the Superette." Rachel's smile broadened. "Tell me he called to ask you out."

"I'm not exactly sure what he did."

Shannon slowed her steps as the two women strolled down the sidewalk of the quaint community with its cute little shops with canopied frontage and large pots of flowers. "He said he had a proposition for me."

A mischievous gleam sparked in Rachel's eyes. "What kind of proposition?"

Shannon swatted her friend's arm and laughed. "Not that kind."

"Don't be so sure." Rachel gave her an admiring glance. "You're a hottie, too. He'd be a fool not to be interested. And that man didn't look like anyone's fool."

"Thanks for that." Still, Shannon held no such illusions. If guys thought of her at all, it was as a buddy. She was twenty-five and had only had two boyfriends. Hardly a guy-magnet. "But remember, his home is in England. I want a nice local guy. Is that too much to ask?"

To Shannon's surprise, Rachel didn't go for the flippant

response. Instead Rachel's dark brows pulled together in thought. Her friend was a strikingly pretty woman, tall with big blue eyes and long hair so dark it looked almost black.

Though they were good friends, so much of Rachel was still a mystery. Sometimes when she turned serious and got this faraway look in her eyes, Shannon could only wonder what she was thinking.

"I love it here, too," Rachel admitted. "I can't imagine living anywhere else. So when you find that nice local guy, make sure he has a friend."

"Will do. Just don't hold your breath."

Shannon stopped short of telling Rachel if her friend was back in Austin, she'd have men beating her door down. She still didn't fully understand what had caused Rachel to leave Austin and move to Horseback Hollow. But in the five years that Rachel had been in town, she'd become part of the community.

"I'm not giving up hope. And you shouldn't either. Look at Quinn," Rachel continued. "Amelia shows up in Horseback Hollow and—boom—she and Quinn fall in love."

Amelia Fortune Chesterfield had come to Horseback Hollow last year for a wedding and had a romantic fling with cowboy Quinn Drummond. Now they were married with a baby girl. It was their baby shower that loomed on the horizon.

"That whole thing was like a made-for-TV movie," Shannon admitted. "But really, how often does that kind of thing happen, especially in a town the size of Horseback Hollow?"

"The fact is, oh ye of little faith, almost anything is possible. Hey, Mr. Oliver Fortune Hayes could fall in love with you, give up his home in London and the two of you could live happily ever after right here."

Shannon paused in front of a bakery, inhaling the scent of freshly baked chocolate chip cookies. "Have you seen a pig fly?"

"Pigs don't fly," Rachel said automatically.

"Exactly right," Shannon agreed. "Until they do, your little scenario isn't going to happen."

Oliver glanced at the Patek Philippe watch on his wrist. His new living room was so small he could cross it in several long strides, which did nothing to dissipate his agitation.

He'd asked Miss Shannon Singleton to come over as soon as possible. That was precisely one hour and forty-five minutes ago. Oliver wasn't used to his requests being ignored.

Of course, as she didn't work for him, Miss Singleton was under no obligation to comply. Still, she'd promised to come as soon as she was able.

Another full hour passed. Ollie was sitting in his high chair, eating a snack of yogurt and apple slices, when Oliver heard the sound of a vehicle coming up the gravel drive.

Barnaby's head jerked up. He let out a surprisingly deep woof, then raced to the front door, tail wagging.

Oliver tousled his son's light brown hair. "Be right back."

His hand was already on the doorknob when the knock sounded.

Looking decidedly windblown, Shannon stood on the porch, holding her flapping purse firmly against her waist as the strong breeze continued to pummel her. Her shoulder-length brown hair whipped around her pretty face and he realized her lips reminded him of plump, ripe strawberries.

He wondered if they'd taste as good as they looked.

She cleared her throat. "May I come in?"

"Of course." Pulling his gaze from her lips, he stepped back and opened the door wider to allow her to pass.

"Whew." She stopped at the edge of the living room to push her hair out of her face. "It's like a hurricane out there."

"Hurricane?" The wind couldn't possibly be over thirty knots.

She laughed. "A figure of speech. If there's a hurricane in the gulf, the only thing we get this far inland is rain. And that's usually in the fall."

Oliver found himself intrigued. Most women of his acquaintance would never think to appear at a requested meeting dressed in blue jeans and a white cotton shirt. Yet, he was oddly drawn to her. It didn't hurt that she smelled terrific, like vanilla.

Yes, the beastly day was definitely on the upswing. "I appreciate you coming on such short notice."

"I'm sorry it took so long." She smiled up at him with such charming sweetness he found himself returning her smile and taking her arm as they strolled to the kitchen.

"You're here now. That's what counts." He resisted the urge to brush back a strand of hair from her face, even as he inhaled the pleasing scent that wafted around her.

"My friend Rachel and I went to a movie in Vicker's Corners. That's where we were when you called. Then we went and got coffee at one of the little specialty shops. This time, we got ice cream, too. I told Rachel we shouldn't. I mean we had a big lunch, but—"

He did his best to process her rapid-fire speech but it was as if she was speaking a foreign language. Apparently cueing in to his glazed look, she broke off and laughed without a hint of self-consciousness.

"I'm babbling." She laughed again. "Which I sometimes do when I'm nervous."

"I make you nervous?"

A bright pink rose up her neck. "A little."

Truly puzzled now, he cocked his head. "Why?"

"You're different from the men I know, the guys in this town."

"My brothers live here. I'm not different from them."

"I'm not well acquainted with your family. At least not with the ones from England."

"Hopefully that will change." Oliver gestured to the refrigerator. "May I get you something to drink?"

"Thanks. I'm fine." She moved to Ollie's side, the dog like a little shadow at her feet. Taking a seat at the table near the child, she smiled and picked up a piece of the apple. "This looks yummy."

The toddler's fingers closed around the apple slice. Her smile flashed with delight when he put it into his mouth and began to chew.

Oliver considered offering her something to eat, but rations were in short supply at the moment. He really needed to make a trip into town to the grocery shop they called the Superette.

"You said you had a proposition for me, Mr. Fortune Hayes?"

She was direct. Oliver admired that quality. Spared all the posturing.

"I'd like you to help me find a nanny for Ollie."

Shannon leaned back in her chair and studied him for several seconds before speaking. "I thought you hired an agency in Lubbock to do that for you. That's the buzz around town."

Jensen had warned him there were no secrets in Horseback Hollow. "Their efforts so far have been disappointing."

"You've been here two days."

"It's difficult to get work done when you're caring for a child."

Unexpectedly, Shannon laughed; a delightful sound that reminded him of bells ringing. "I don't think any parent would contradict that statement."

"The fact is, Miss Singleton—"

"Shannon," she reminded him.

"Shannon." He found the name pleasant on his tongue. "My business is a demanding one. While I'm happy to come and spend time with my family, I need to stay involved."

"What is it you do?"

"I run a brokerage house." It would be bragging to say more, to tell her that his firm was one of the top ones in London. Besides, it had no relevance to the current conversation.

"Oh."

"The point is I need to find someone immediately. Of course, not just anyone will do. Ollie's happiness and welfare is paramount. The women the agency has sent so far were totally inappropriate. This has caused me to doubt the adequacy of the agency's screening process."

"How were they inappropriate?" Shannon knew he'd acquired the services of the premier placement agency in Lubbock. To hear he was dissatisfied so quickly surprised her.

"The first woman hadn't been informed this was a live-in position." Oliver snatched from the air the piece of apple Ollie had tried to fling to a waiting Barnaby. "Interviewing her was a complete waste of my time."

"Probably an oversight," Shannon said diplomatically. "What else?"

"The next woman found the accommodations—" he hesitated for a second before continuing "—substandard. That didn't concern me because I found her supercilious attitude unacceptable."

"Many live-in nannies—" Shannon chose her words carefully since the lodging they were referring to was owned by her father "—require a private bath."

"I completely understand her concern," Oliver said briskly. "I'm not looking forward to sharing the lavatory either. I'd hoped the salary I was offering and the fact that it wouldn't be a long-term placement would make that fact more palatable."

"It must be difficult living in a home that is so far below your circumstances."

He appeared to ignore her dry tone. "This home and Horseback Hollow may not be where I'd choose to live forever, but for the short term both are adequate."

Shannon knew he was being kind and exceedingly tactful. But his comment only served to remind her that Oliver Fortune Hayes wouldn't be like his sister, Amelia, or his brother Jensen, who'd come to Horseback Hollow and not only fallen in love with a local but with the town and its people, as well.

She had to keep that in mind. Despite the ooh la la factor, any relationship with Oliver would be a dead-end street.

Chapter Three

Oliver found himself enjoying his conversation with Shannon. She was obviously an intelligent woman who appeared to truly care about his situation.

"I asked Amelia for names since Amber and Jensen were fresh out of ideas." Oliver paused and tilted his head. "Are you certain I can't get you a refreshment?"

Shannon smiled. She had quite a lovely one. While her features were too strong to be considered classically beautiful, there was an arresting nature to her face that made a man—even one who'd sworn off women temporarily to focus on his son—take a second look.

Though he must admit, he couldn't recall the last time he'd seen a woman in denim and cotton. Not to mention cowboy boots. The pants hugged her slender figure like a glove, and the shirt, though not tight, hinted at underlying curves. Yes, she was striking indeed.

"I guess I could take a cup of tea, if it's not too much trouble."

He was so focused on her lips that it took him a second to process. "No trouble at all."

Oliver was putting the kettle on the stove when the doorbell rang.

"Would you like me to get that?" Even as she asked, Shannon was already rising to her feet with a fluid grace comparable to any of the ladies he knew back in London.

"Thank you, yes." Oliver pulled his gaze from her backside and gave Ollie a biscuit. His son squealed with delight.

He heard Shannon speak, then recognized his brother's voice.

Jensen strolled into the room, dressed casually—for him—in brown trousers and a cream-colored polo shirt. There was curiosity in his eyes when his brother's gaze slid between him and Shannon. "I didn't realize the two of you were acquainted."

"Shannon showed me around this lovely home," Oliver announced.

"That's, ah, correct." Shannon, who'd appeared relaxed only moments before, now appeared ready to bolt.

The fact puzzled Oliver. He'd been under the impression that while Shannon and Jensen weren't well acquainted, they were on good terms.

"Will you have a cup?" Oliver asked his brother. "I have Fortnum & Mason."

Jensen's smile gave Oliver his answer, while Shannon's brows pulled together.

"Fortnum & Mason is a popular British tea manufacturer. They have a Smoky Earl Grey blend that Oliver—and almost everyone in the family—prefers," Jensen explained before Oliver could open his mouth.

"I'm sure it's delicious, but I'll have to pass." Shannon

appeared to make a great show of looking at her watch. "We can talk another time, Oliver. I have plans and I'm sure you and your brother have a lot to discuss."

Oliver's heart gave an odd lurch. He surprised himself by crossing the room, taking her arm and leading her back to her seat at the table. "Nonsense. You're staying for tea."

"Down," Ollie called out. "Want down."

"I can get—" Shannon began.

Oliver held up a hand, then fixed his gaze on his son. "What do you say?"

Ollie stared at him with innocent blue eyes before his mouth widened into a grin. "Pease."

"Good man." Oliver lifted his son down from the high chair.

Jensen exchanged a look with Shannon. "Amazing."

Shannon cocked her head, but before Jensen could explain, Oliver looked up from wiping Ollie's hands.

"Nothing amazing about it. Child rearing is no different from running a successful business enterprise. Rules and order are essential." Oliver shifted his gaze to Shannon. "My brother expected me to be a bumbling feckwit incapable of rearing my son."

Oliver pulled out a bin containing an assortment of toys, placing several before Ollie on the rug within eyeshot of the kitchen table. The whistling teakettle brought him back to the stove, where he produced three cups of the steaming brew in short order.

"Surely he's seen you in action before?" Shannon cradled the "I Love Texas" mug in her hands with an unexpected reverence.

"Oliver only recently gained custody of Ollie," Jensen explained. "After Diane…"

Jensen stopped and slanted Oliver an apologetic glance.

In their family, private matters weren't usually discussed in the presence of a guest.

"Diane was my ex-wife," Oliver explained. "The divorce was already in process when Ollie was born. Because I believed a child—a baby especially—needed his mother, I didn't fight her for custody. She recently died in a car accident."

"She shouldn't have been out that night." Jensen's voice rose and anger flashed in his eyes. "She should—"

"Enough."

The quietly spoken word was enough to stop Jensen's potential tirade in its tracks.

"She was Ollie's mother." Looking back, the person Oliver blamed most was himself. He should have paid more attention. He should have known that Diane was spending more time with her new boyfriend than with Ollie. "The accident occurred fairly recently."

He felt Shannon's hand on his arm, looked up to find her soft eyes filled with compassion. "I'm sorry for your loss."

"We'd been divorced over a year."

"You were also once married to her. That means you once loved her." She gave his forearm a squeeze, then removed her hand.

Oliver nodded briskly.

Diane hadn't wasted any time finding another man once the baby was born. She'd been with yet another man when she died. That's why the sadness he'd experienced upon hearing of her passing had blindsided him. He finally accepted it was understandable, given this was a woman he'd once known and loved.

Jensen steepled his fingers and his gaze settled on Shannon. "I understand you work for your father."

"I do." She sipped her tea and her smile told Oliver she found it pleasing. "The Triple S is a large spread. I do mostly administrative work, but in a pinch I'm able to do just about anything—feed cattle, vaccinate, castrate…"

"Good Lord." The words popped from Oliver's lips before he could stop them.

"You're in the Wild West now, brother." Jensen grinned. "Oh, and before I forget, I brought you some more names of possible nannies for Ollie. These are from Amelia since you didn't appear happy with any of the ones Amber and I suggested."

"I'm very particular when it comes to my son," Oliver said without apology.

Jensen took a sip of tea, then lifted the mug higher to read the inscription—"This Ain't My First Rodeo." His lips twitched and he shook his head before taking another drink. Seconds later he reached into his pocket and pulled out a sheet of paper. "The latest list."

"Perfect," Oliver pronounced. "We'll take care of this right now."

Jensen tilted his head back. "How do you propose to do that?"

"Miss Singleton knows everyone in the area." Oliver smiled at Shannon. "She and I will go through the names over dinner and decide which ones to interview."

"I'm afraid that won't be possible." Shannon set down her mug, the flash of irritation in her eyes at odds with her easy tone. "I have plans."

"Break them," Oliver ordered. "This is more important. A child's welfare is at stake."

The men in Shannon's family often told their friends that she was a contradiction: a purring kitten and a ready-to-strike rattler. The consensus seemed to be it was best not to push her too far.

The good humor drained from Shannon's body. Did the

rich and powerful Oliver Fortune Hayes really think he could, with a cavalier wave of his hand, dismiss her plans for the evening?

There was no reason for him to know that those plans were fluid. Several friends planned to eat and drink their way through platters of nachos and bottles of Corona beer at the Hollows Cantina during happy hour. They'd told her to join them if she was free.

But as Shannon opened her mouth to reiterate she had plans, his words gave her pause. As much as she didn't want Oliver to think he could bring her to heel with a single wave of those elegant fingers, she wanted him to find a suitable nanny for Ollie.

You'd think after growing up with four younger siblings— and years spent babysitting—she should be tired of children. But she loved them. Not just the small ones. She even got a kick out of the often obnoxious teenagers from Lubbock who came out to ride horses as part of a Country Connection program.

Ollie was such a cute little guy and he'd recently lost his mother...

"Shannon." Oliver reached across the table and took her hand. "Please. I need your help." His tone was softer this time.

Heat rose up her arm. For a second she forgot how to speak. She licked her lips. When his eyes darkened, her resistance melted into a liquid pool.

"I'd love to stay and chat, but Amber is expecting me." Jensen attempted to hide his grin by raising the cup to his lips for one last swallow. "It appears you two have a lot to, uh, discuss."

Shannon flushed. "Be sure to tell Amber hello from me."

"I will give her your regards." Jensen gave a slight bow

of his head, all serious now. One hundred percent British. He turned and handed Oliver the promised list. "The names."

"Thank you." Oliver took the list in his left hand, extended his right. The two men shook.

Shannon blinked at the civilized gesture. She tried to imagine her brothers shaking hands and...couldn't. Punching each other, heck yes. That occurred on a daily basis.

Because the men were standing, she also rose to her feet. Jensen shook her hand before he left.

With a resigned sigh, Shannon turned to Oliver. She had to admit she was curious whom Amelia had recommended. She gazed pointedly at the list dangling from his fingers. "May I see it?"

With paper in hand, Shannon wandered back to the table and sat. Taking a gulp of tea, she narrowed her gaze and scanned the names.

After putting down a few more toys for Ollie, Oliver took a seat across from her.

"What do you think?" he asked when several seconds had passed. "Any good possibilities?"

Shannon laid the paper on the table and sat back. "Do you want tactful? Or honest?"

Oliver's gaze lingered on her face, and a curious energy filled the air. An invisible web of attraction wrapped around them. When he leaned forward, Shannon was sure he was going to kiss her.

Unable to move, she held her breath and stared into those brilliant blue eyes.

His lips were a heartbeat away when little Ollie let out a high-pitched squeal. Shannon turned her head just in time to see him gleefully knock down the stack of blocks.

Though he'd recently lost his mother, the child appeared happy and content, with the dog sitting upright beside him.

Right now all was well in his life, and that warmed her heart. But the little boy's world could quickly take a nose-dive if Oliver hired any of the women Amelia had suggested.

She shifted her gaze back to Oliver. The moment had vanished. It was almost as if it had never existed. This made Shannon wonder if it had been simply wishful thinking on her part.

"Quinn isn't much for gossip and your sister is relatively new to Horseback Hollow." Shannon strove to keep her tone matter-of-fact. "I grew up here. I keep my ear to the ground."

The expression seemed to puzzle Oliver. His dark brows pulled together.

"I know everything that goes on in this town," she clarified. "Things your sister and even her husband might not know."

Understanding filled his eyes. "Tell me."

"Will you keep it confidential?" Though Shannon liked to have the scoop, she wasn't a gossip. Okay, not much of one. The only reason she was considering sharing what she knew with Oliver was to protect Ollie.

"Most certainly."

Based on what Shannon had observed, Oliver appeared to be an honorable man who loved his son and wanted the best for him.

Hoping she wasn't making a mistake dissing women his sister had recommended, Shannon went through the names on the list one by one. By the time they'd gone through three, Ollie had tired of his toys and was rubbing his eyes and whining. Barnaby sprawled on a nearby rug, snoring lightly.

"Let's break for a few minutes." Oliver rose to his feet.

"I need to change Ollie's nappy and put him down for a kip."

He inclined his head, and she knew what he was asking without him saying a word.

"I'll wait."

"Your dinner plans?"

"No worries." Though it was almost five and the start of happy hour was seconds away, Shannon was no longer in a hurry to leave. "While you're taking care of Ollie, I'll make us another cup of that delicious tea."

"Thank you."

When he and his son disappeared down the hall, Shannon sent a quick text to her friends, canceling her appearance, then put the kettle on. By the time he returned from the bedroom, the tea was ready.

"How is he?" She placed the two cups on the table.

"Dry and sleeping." He gestured toward the steaming tea. "Thank you for that...and for staying."

"I let my friends know I'd be late." She raised a hand when he started to protest. "I want to finish this with you. We only have two names left."

He studied her for a long moment before dropping his gaze down to the list and pointing. "What about this one?"

"Sally Steinacher drinks." When Oliver opened his mouth, she continued. "Not just socially. She has a problem. The family did an intervention last year and she went through treatment, but she's fallen off the wagon. Last week when I was in Vicker's Corners, I spotted her coming out of a liquor store with a sack."

"Perhaps she was buying for a friend or a family member," Oliver suggested.

Shannon gave him a pitying glance. "What kind of friend or relative would send an alcoholic to buy them liquor? Even if someone were that stupid, Rachel and I ran into her later on the street and we both smelled alcohol on her breath."

Oliver lined through her name with a single precise stroke of his Montblanc pen, the same way he'd done with the previous three names. "We've now reached the last person on the list. Is Cissy Jirovec a possibility?"

The hopeful look in his eye vanished when Shannon shook her head.

"She used to live in Horseback Hollow. Cissy calls Vicker's Corners home now. She's a nice person and I know she did a lot of babysitting while she was growing up."

"Then what's the issue?"

There was something about having those vivid blue eyes focused on her that Shannon found unsettling. "The problem isn't with Cissy. It's with her boyfriend."

"I wouldn't be hiring him."

"Wayne used to live in Horseback Hollow. He has a bad temper."

"What does her relationship with this man have to do with her suitability for the position?"

"Wayne has a child from a relationship with another woman in Lubbock. Several years ago he lost his temper and broke his daughter's arm. The doctors in the ER found other healed injuries when they examined the little girl. He was charged with felony child abuse. I read all about it in the Lubbock paper."

"He did this to his own child?"

"He did." Shannon nodded solemnly. "I would hope Cissy wouldn't invite Wayne over while she was watching Ollie. But if Ollie were my son, I wouldn't take the risk."

Just as he had with the previous four names, Oliver drew a line through Cissy's name. With one hand he crumpled the sheet of paper.

"I might have hired one of these women." There was a look of restrained horror on his face.

"On the surface they look good. But, don't despair. The placement agency you're working with is top-notch. They'll do a good job of screening the candidates for you." She offered him a reassuring smile. "You'll find that right someone soon."

Oliver shook his head. "I think I've just found her. I want you to watch Oliver."

"Pardon me?"

"Name your price."

"Mr. Fortune Hayes—"

"Oliver," he interrupted, offering her a smile that turned her bones to liquid. "If we're going to be living under the same roof, it makes sense to be on a first-name basis."

Her breath caught in her throat. "What are you saying?"

"We should be on a first-name basis. Don't you agree?"

"I—I suppose."

"Splendid." The smile that split his face made him look almost boyish. "Shall we shake on it…Shannon?"

Chapter Four

"Shake on what? I haven't agreed to any deal." Shannon stuck her hands behind her back. Thank goodness the words came out casual and offhand.

"Smart woman. It's always best to discuss terms on the front end." He leaned forward in a companionable gesture, resting his forearms on the table.

The gesture somehow made him seem more approachable and appealing. Although if he got much more appealing, Shannon might jump him and rip off that pristine white shirt and perfectly knotted tie.

When Shannon didn't speak, he simply smiled. "You obviously know your negotiating techniques. Okay, I'll toss out an amount."

"We're not negotiating," Shannon protested. "Look, Mr. Fortune Hay—"

"Oliver," he said, once more not playing fair by flashing that enticing smile. "We decided on first names."

"Okay, Oliver." Shannon raked back her hair with her fingers, her heart pounding. Why did she feel as if she was in a race she was destined to lose? A race that, in some ways, she wanted to lose? "I—"

Before she could say more, he tossed out a number that had her forgetting what she'd been about to say.

"I believe that's a fair offer."

"Per...?" She really didn't want to say per month if he meant every two weeks, but it was an amazing sum of money either way.

"Week."

Shannon tried to control her expression by counting to ten in her head. The amount was five times what she'd been making in Lubbock. She swallowed past her suddenly dry throat and shifted in her seat. "If you're offering to pay that much, I'm surprised you don't have women—and men—beating down the door to work for you."

"That's not the salary the agency suggested. They told me the going rate in the area and I agreed to it." His gaze searched her eyes. "I'm a businessman, Shannon. I'm willing to pay for quality. It's as simple as that."

Shannon never considered she could be bought, but then again she'd never been offered so much money for a position she knew she'd enjoy. Working for her father was fine, but he really didn't need her. Little Ollie did.

Oliver turned his head slightly to the side. "What do you say?"

Shannon wiped suddenly sweaty palms on her jeans. "Before we discuss salary any further, I'd like to know your expectations."

He nodded approvingly and studied her for another long moment.

"Timewise, London is six hours ahead of Horseback Hollow." He gestured with an open palm to the clock on the wall in the shape of a rooster. "This means that much of my business will be conducted very early in the morning. That's why living in is nonnegotiable."

"I could come first thing in the morning, say at six a.m." She'd almost said five, but that was her father's favorite time to roll out of bed, not hers.

"That won't work." Oliver tapped a finger on the table. "If I'm speaking with a client at two a.m. and Ollie starts crying and needs attention, I need someone here who can tend to him."

"He could spend the night with me at my parents' home." The words came out in a rush, before she even considered what her folks might think about having a toddler underfoot. All she knew was the idea of being under the same roof with Oliver Fortune Hayes night after night was...disturbing. "That way, you could conduct business without any interruptions at all."

When she finished speaking, Oliver shook his head. The set of his jaw said there would be no changing his mind. "I want Ollie's schedule to be disrupted as little as possible. If I hadn't already canceled other trips to see my family, I'd have canceled this one and remained in London. Ollie has experienced more changes in the past few months than any little boy should have to face."

"You care about him."

Oliver looked perplexed. "Did you think I didn't?"

Well, she wanted to say, *sometimes you treat him like just one more thing in your life you need to handle.* But she knew that wasn't being fair. Her interaction with Oliver and his son had been minimal.

"No, of course not." Shannon blew out a breath. "You're probably right about not injecting more change into his life."

He relaxed in his chair. "Any other concerns you'd like to discuss?"

Shannon cleared her throat. "What about meal preparation, laundry and housecleaning duties? Would those be something you'd expect from me?"

"Negotiable."

"I would need time off."

"I'm not a slave driver, Shannon." His lips lifted in a boyish smile before he became all business again. "At a minimum I would require you to be here between the hours of midnight to noon, Monday through Friday. However, I'd prefer that during the working week you remain on duty until six p.m. That would allow me to have some sleep knowing Ollie is safe under your care."

Though he was proposing some pretty long hours, she *would* have every evening free. Other than Rachel, most of her friends worked eight-to-five jobs, and this really would be no different. "What about weekends?"

"Those days are yours."

She tapped her index finger against her bottom lip. "It's tempting."

"I'd like you to start immediately."

"You're getting ahead of yourself, Bucko." The word, commonly used by Shannon and her sibs, slipped out before her lips could trap it and swallow it whole.

"Bucko?" Oliver raised one dark brow. "I don't believe I'm familiar with the term."

His lips twitched ever so slightly.

Sheesh, the guy was appealing. And that was part of her concern.

Shannon jerked her gaze from those lips and squared her shoulders. There was no getting around it. The elephant in the room had to be addressed. "There's one thing we haven't yet discussed. How you respond may be the difference between my accepting your offer or respectfully declining it."

Oliver's eyes turned flat. He folded his hands before him on the table, his gaze never wavering from her face. "You have my undivided attention."

The fact that Oliver was being so businesslike should have made it easier to spit out the words stuck in her throat. But somehow, having those blue eyes focused so intently on her made her feel like a schoolgirl about to admit to a crush. Dear God, what if she'd only imagined the chemistry between them?

Shannon shifted in her seat and hesitated, despite knowing there was nothing to do at this point but take a deep breath and plunge ahead.

She focused her gaze on a spot over his left shoulder. "Ever since we've met, I've noticed this crazy kind of electricity between us. That's why I think it's important we agree up front to keep things strictly platonic between us. Giving in to the attraction would only complicate the situation."

She was out of breath by the time she finished. Had he been able to understand what she was trying to say? She'd spoken so fast—too fast—the words tripping over each other in her haste to get them out.

"Electricity?"

Of course if he was going to pick one word to focus on, it would naturally be that one. But it was the twinkle in those blue eyes that had her jerking to her feet, a hot flush shooting up her neck.

"Forget it. Forget I said anything. This isn't going to work." To her horror, her voice shook slightly.

It wasn't the hint of amusement in his eyes that had gotten to her. It was the frustration of not being able to make herself heard. Of her concerns and feelings being summarily dismissed.

That's how it had been with Jerry the Jerk. No matter how many different ways she'd told him to back off—that she wasn't interested—he never heard her.

Because he didn't want to hear what I had to say. Because I didn't matter.

As emotions flooded her, Shannon whirled toward the door.

She'd taken only a step or two when Oliver grabbed her arm, his expression contrite.

"I didn't mean to wind you up." He loosened his grip but didn't let go. "You have my word as a gentleman that I will never take advantage of you while you're under my roof and in my employ."

Shannon blew out a shaky breath and swayed slightly, conscious of his hand on her arm. He stood an arm's breadth away, near enough for the intoxicating scent of his cologne to tease her nostrils and make her want to lean close.

Step back, she told herself. She needed to put some distance between her and Oliver. That way she could think. That way she could breathe.

But her feet were as heavy and unmoving as if rooted in concrete. At that moment Shannon didn't have the energy—or the desire—to move.

Instead she tilted her head back and once again found herself drowning in the shockingly blue depths of Oliver's eyes.

Oliver stepped toward her, hand outstretched.

The heat in his gaze ignited a fire in her belly.

A zillion butterflies fluttered in her chest. Shannon moistened her lips and, as she caught another whiff of his cologne, reconsidered her hardline stance of only a moment ago.

One kiss.

What would really be wrong with one little kiss?

After all, people shook hands all the time to seal a deal. How would this be any different? Even as the rational piece of her brain still capable of cognizant thought told her it was indeed *very different*, she extended her hand.

Shannon waited for him to take her fingers and tug her to him. Waited for that magic moment when he would enfold her in a warm embrace before covering her mouth with his…

Her lips were already tingling with anticipation when his hand closed over hers and he gave it a decisive shake. "To new beginnings."

Even as a tsunami-sized wave of disappointment washed over her, Shannon forced herself to breathe and made her lips curve in an easy smile.

Regroup, she told herself.

Her father always said actions spoke louder than words. By his actions, Oliver had shown he was a man of his word. A man she could trust. There was something even more important Shannon had learned today.

She had more to fear from herself than from him.

Happy Hour at the Hollows Cantina had been going for close to two hours by the time Shannon strolled through the front door. She wasn't surprised to find standing-room-only in the bar area.

Her friends tried to squeeze her in at their table, but even if she could have located a spare chair, there was no room for one more.

"That's okay." Shannon waved a hand in the direction of the bar. "I'll just mingle."

"I'm coming with you." Rachel's heels had barely hit the shiny hardwood before her chair was snatched away.

Good old Rachel, Shannon thought with a warm rush of affection. She could always count on her.

The two women wove their way through the crowd, stopping every few feet to chat with friends and acquaintances while keeping an eye out for a couple of empty spots at the bar. They finally snagged two stools when a young couple got up abruptly and hurried off, hands all over each other.

"Get a room," someone yelled, and laughter rippled through the crowd.

A bartender approached to wipe the counter and take their order.

"The nachos are my treat," Shannon announced.

Rachel narrowed her gaze. "What's got you feeling so generous?"

"Tonight is a special occasion." Shannon smiled her thanks as the bartender placed a bottle of Corona beer sporting a wedge of lime in front of her. Before he rushed off he assured her the nachos would be out shortly. "We're celebrating."

The half-finished bottle Rachel had brought with her from the table paused midway to her lips and a smile blossomed on her mouth. "You know I adore happy news. Clue me in. What are we celebrating?"

Shannon raised the beer in a mock toast. Initially she'd been hesitant about accepting Oliver's offer. But now she felt confident of her ability to withstand temptation. "My new job."

Rachel's smile froze. Then she clinked her bottle against the one Shannon held and sputtered out her congratulations.

"Thanks. I'm superjazzed." The position was all about

Ollie, she reassured herself. She had no doubt she and the boy would get along splendidly. Shannon would not think about the way her heart hammered whenever Oliver was near.

"When did they call you?"

The quietly spoken question came out of nowhere. Shannon blinked and focused on her friend. "Who?"

"The person who contacted you about the Fortune Foundation job." Rachel cleared her throat. "When did you get the good news?"

The bartender, a thirtysomething-year-old with a shaved head, set a plate of loaded nachos in front of them.

"I never thought they'd choose someone this soon," Rachel continued before Shannon had a chance to respond. "But, hey, if it couldn't be me, I'm happy it was you."

"This isn't the foundation job. They won't let us know until the end of the month, remember?" Shannon picked up a chip dripping with cheese and nibbled. "I'm going to be a nanny to Oliver Fortune Hayes's son. It's short-term but the position pays extremely well."

"Oh." The tightness on Rachel's face eased. "When do you start?"

"I move in Sunday night." Shannon popped the nacho into her mouth. "I asked him for a few days to get my stuff together and my bags packed."

"You're moving in with him?" Rachel's voice rose.

Shannon quickly explained about the time difference and the need to be there to watch Ollie while Oliver was conducting business.

"How did your folks take the news?"

A twinkle of amusement danced in Rachel's eyes. Like most Horseback Hollow natives, her friend knew Shannon's parents were a bit on the conservative side.

Shannon grimaced, not looking forward to that conversation. "They don't know. Not yet. I was at Oliver's place until I came here. All I can do is assure them it's strictly business between us."

"Easy peasy." Rachel waved a dismissive hand. "Five minutes in his presence and they'll see it couldn't be anything but business."

Shannon frowned. "What makes you say that?"

"Think about how he stands, so straight and tall. It's like he's got a poker up his a—" Rachel stopped abruptly when she saw Pastor Dunbrook two stools away. She lowered her voice. "I'm just saying that while Oliver may look smokin' hot—and sound just as good as he looks—he has that British thing going."

"British thing?"

"Stiff upper lip and all that. Jolly good and tally-ho." Rachel tapped two fingers against her lips. "Kissing him would probably be like kissing a corpse."

As if Rachel's attempt at a proper British accent wasn't hilarious enough, her describing Oliver as a cold fish made Shannon laugh.

"What's so funny?" Rachel tilted her head, and a speculative gleam shone in her eyes. "Have you already kissed him?"

"Ra-chel." The name was said with just the right touch of injured emotion and appeared to allay her friend's suspicions. "I barely know the man."

"That wouldn't stop me if I was interested in a guy."

"Well, I'm not interested in Oliver, not in that way. This is strictly a business arrangement."

"Then why did you laugh?"

"Because I don't see Oliver as being a cold fish."

"Yeah, right."

"No. Seriously. He's simply…British."

Rachel rolled her eyes and swiped a nacho off the plate.

"Okay, so maybe he's a bit uptight," Shannon admitted. "But it wouldn't take much to loosen him up."

"You go for it, sister." Rachel's red lips focused on something in the distance then curved upward in a sly smile. "In fact, there's no better time to start than right now."

"Other than I'm occupied, enjoying this scrumptious plate of nachos and—" Shannon lifted the Corona "—this ice-cold beer with you. Oliver, on the other hand, is—"

"Right behind you."

"What?"

"Turn," Rachel ordered.

Shannon swiveled on the bar stool. She inhaled sharply and her heart began pumping in time to the sexy salsa beat.

The man she'd been chatting with less than an hour earlier stood in the lobby. Ollie stood fidgeting at his side while Oliver chatted amiably with Wendy Fortune Mendoza and Marcos Mendoza, owners of the cantina. Wendy, looking as stylish as ever in a wrap dress of bright red with matching five-inch heels, clasped the hand of her three-year-old daughter, MaryAnne.

Even as Shannon's eyes were drawn to MaryAnne's adorable pink-and-white-striped dress, she couldn't help noticing the way Marcos's hand rested lovingly on his wife's shoulder or how hot Oliver looked.

He'd changed his clothes, wearing yet another dark suit but this time coupled with a gray shirt and charcoal tie. Odd he hadn't mentioned he had plans for the evening. He certainly hadn't acted as if he was in a rush for her to leave. Quite the contrary.

"Time to start warming up the iceberg," Rachel said in a low tone.

"Saying hello would be the polite thing to do," Shannon agreed, ignoring Rachel's snort of laughter.

Placing her Corona bottle down, Shannon hopped off the stool and pulled a small round mirror from her bag. Before taking a step, she touched up her lipstick, then flashed Rachel a smile. "Back in five."

Rachel lifted a nacho heavy with beef and cheese and gestured to the platter. "Just warning you, these may be all gone when you get back."

"I will return to find both the nachos *and* my seat waiting." Shannon pointed at her friend and spoke in an ominous voice suitable for any horror flick. "Or you will pay the price."

"No guarantee, Chickadee." Rachel peered over the Corona bottle at Shannon and those baby blues twinkled. "If some sexy cowboy wants that stool, those chips or me, I'm sayin' yes."

Shannon ignored the warning and turned, anticipation fueling her steps as she headed across the hardwood floor toward Oliver.

Chapter Five

Though Oliver hadn't had the pleasure of meeting Wendy Fortune Mendoza before tonight, he was well aware she was one of his Texas cousins. The minute he walked into the Hollows Cantina, she greeted him warmly. Since she and her husband owned the cantina, Oliver assumed Wendy and Marcos were cohosting the last-minute party his mother, Josephine, had organized.

But Wendy informed him that she and Marcos wouldn't be able to stay. Even though they couldn't attend, they'd made the restaurant's private room available for the impromptu dinner.

"I'm happy to have the opportunity to meet you." Marcos, a tall man in a perfectly tailored suit with piercing dark eyes, gave Oliver's hand a firm shake.

From what Oliver had heard, Marcos was a savvy businessman, yet it was clear, seeing him with his wife and daughter, that family was also important to him. A man would have to be blind not to notice the loving way Marcos's gaze lingered on Wendy.

"I don't know if you heard but I've secured lodging at a ranch house on the Singleton property. I'll be there for the duration of my stay in Horseback Hollow." Oliver dropped his gaze and shot Ollie a warning glance when the child began tugging on his hand. "Stop by sometime. Bring your daughter. Ollie seems to enjoy being around other children."

"Wonderful. I'll call you this week and we'll set something up." Wendy started to say more but shifted her attention and smiled brilliantly. "Shannon. It's been ages."

Oliver turned to see Wendy give his new nanny a quick hug. She slipped an arm through Shannon's and lifted her gaze to Oliver. "I'm not sure if you've had a chance to meet Shep's daughter—"

"Introductions are unnecessary." Oliver offered Shannon a warm smile. "Miss Singleton and I are well acquainted."

Wendy exchanged a glance with her husband.

"Just this afternoon Shannon agreed to be Ollie's live-in nanny," Oliver announced.

Astonishment rippled across his cousin's pretty face. "Why, that's wonderful."

"Live-in?" Marcos's dark eyes narrowed. "Your father approves of this plan?"

"I'm twenty-five, Marcos," Shannon said drily. "I hardly need my father's okay."

"He's your father," Marcos said pointedly.

"Living in is necessary because of the time difference between here and London." Shannon quickly explained the circumstances, ignoring Marcos's disapproving glance and focusing on Wendy instead.

"Because of that six-hour difference, most of Oliver's

business will be conducted during the overnight hours," Shannon continued before Oliver could add anything. "As a toddler, Ollie can't be counted on to sleep through the night."

"We know all about sleepless nights." Wendy shot a teasing glance at her husband. "Remember when MaryAnne was that age?"

Marcos nodded but his gaze remained troubled.

For the first time, Oliver considered what Shep Singleton would think of his daughter living under the roof of a man he didn't know. Would he understand that it was a simple business arrangement? Or would he worry Oliver might take advantage of Shannon?

Shep had been pleasant and accommodating when Oliver had called to inquire about the house. A personal visit to the Singleton home appeared necessary. Oliver would introduce himself, explain the situation and allay the man's fears before Shannon moved in on Monday.

He was planning his strategy when his mum, Josephine Fortune Chesterfield, breezed through the door, a vision in pale blue silk. Her gray hair, arranged in a chignon, flattered her handsome face. "I'm here. The party can begin."

She extended both hands and moved quickly to him. "Oliver."

"You look lovely as always." He took her hands in his then bent to brush a kiss against her cheek.

"Good evening, Wendy. Marcos." His mother's curious gaze settled on Shannon. "You're Shannon Singleton, Shep and Lilian's daughter. Am I correct?"

"You have an excellent memory, Mrs. Chesterfield." Shannon smiled at his mother. "How are you this evening?"

"Josephine, please. I'm wonderful, now that my son and grandson have joined me in Horseback Hollow."

Ollie made a sound of displeasure when Oliver tightened his hold on the child's hand.

"There's my little darling." Without warning, Josephine scooped Ollie up into her arms.

Startled, the boy stiffened. His eyes widened and his bottom lip began to tremble. Oliver certainly didn't relish snatching Ollie from his mother's arms. But neither did he want his son to start crying and cause a scene in public.

He was rapidly sorting through options when Shannon stepped forward and stroked the child's arm, diverting his attention.

"Hey, Ollie," she said in a gentle, melodious tone. "Remember me from this afternoon?"

Apparently the child did remember. His trembling lips morphed into a wide smile and he extended chubby arms to Shannon.

Instead of taking him from his grandmother as Oliver expected, Shannon clasped his small hands in hers and jiggled them up and down. "Can you tell your grandma your puppy's name?"

Ollie smiled, showing a mouthful of drool and tiny white teeth. "Barn-bee."

"Is Barnaby a nice puppy?" Josephine shot Shannon a grateful smile before refocusing on her grandson, now content in her arms.

As the two continued their corgi conversation, Oliver touched Shannon's arm, drawing her attention to him. "Thanks."

She shot him a wink. "No prob."

Their gazes locked and that electricity she'd mentioned returned to give him a hard jolt.

Blast it all to hell and back. He was not so crass as to be attracted to the nanny. Okay, so perhaps he was…

intrigued. Shannon was different from the London social-
ites he frequently took to the opera and sometimes to bed.

But *intrigued* didn't translate into action. Correction,
wouldn't lead to action. Even if Shannon wasn't his employee, Ollie and managing his business affairs were his
top priority.

Shannon's eyes widened as Fortunes flooded the lobby,
including Oliver's brother Jensen and his fiancée, Amber.
"Why is everyone here? What's the occasion?"

"Mum decided to host a last-minute dinner party. She
invited all the family in the area." Oliver smiled ruefully.
"She didn't want to put my aunt out so she decided to have
it here. She's a bit impulsive, but that's part of her charm."

"How fun. I admire spontaneity." A hint of wistfulness
crept into Shannon's voice. "I'm not spontaneous. You miss
out on a lot when you're always thinking things through."

"So true, my dear," Josephine interjected.

Shannon's cheeks grew pink. Clearly, she hadn't realized that his mother had eyes—and ears—in the back of
her head.

"I was surprised to see you here this evening. I didn't
know—" Oliver stopped, remembering. "That's right. You
told me you had plans."

"I met some friends for happy hour." Shannon glanced
over to the bar.

Oliver followed her gaze. A cowboy sat in the seat she'd
vacated moments before, munching on nachos. Was the
man someone she knew?

Oliver opened his mouth but shut it without speaking.
Not his concern.

Strictly business, he reminded himself.

"It was a pleasure seeing you again, Josephine." Shannon's use of his mum's first name earned an approving
smile. "Enjoy your dinner party and your grandson."

Shannon shifted her gaze to Oliver, and when those brown eyes settled on him, he experienced another punch of awareness.

"Trust me." She lowered her voice to a conspiratorial whisper. "Go with the enchiladas. They're the best."

Unable to resist touching her, Oliver reached over and lightly squeezed her shoulder. "Thank you...for everything."

Shannon smiled and strolled off.

"I thought someone said we were meeting in the party room," a feminine voice said. "But the lobby works for me."

Oliver turned to find a petite dark-haired woman with an angelic face and a wide smile approaching him.

"You probably don't remember me from the other night." The young woman extended her hand. "I'm Gabi Mendoza. We—"

"He remembers you, darlin'." Jude Fortune Jones, another one of Oliver's Horseback Hollow cousins, stepped forward and pressed a kiss on the top of Gabi's head. "No man forgets you."

Gabi flashed her tall blond fiancé an indulgent smile. "Aw, thanks, honey. But Oliver saw a lot of new faces the day he arrived."

Though Oliver was exceedingly good with names and faces, Gabi was correct. With so many relatives to meet, including their spouses and significant others, he appreciated her courtesy. "We didn't have much of a chance to chat the other day."

"Tonight we'll get better acquainted over cowboy caviar," Gabi told him.

Oliver pulled his brows together, completely flummoxed. "Cowboy caviar?"

"It's not really caviar." Jude slanted a glance at his fiancée, who simply smiled cheekily.

"It's actually a type of dip," Gabi explained. "It contains black beans, tomato, avocado, onion, cilantro and corn."

"Interesting," Oliver murmured.

Jude grinned. "Let's just say it's a whole lot more tasty than those nasty fish eggs."

"Oliver has a discerning palate," Jude's brother Christopher Fortune Jones tossed out as he strolled past. "And you, bro, are just a hick from the sticks."

Jude's eyes flashed, but then Gabi wrapped her arms around his neck and pressed her nicely curved body against him. "I like you just the way you are, sweetie pie."

Oliver couldn't decide if he'd just witnessed normal sibling interaction or if there was more behind the tension between the brothers.

"Oh my goodness." Gabi pulled from Jude's arms. "I almost forgot."

The pretty Latina turned to Josephine, who still held her grandson.

"I hope you don't mind. I asked my father to join us tonight. Jude and I had planned to have dinner with him. Then you called and—"

"Orlando is here?" Josephine sounded oddly breathless.

"He's on his way. I hope it's no trouble."

"No trouble at all." Josephine's free hand rose to smooth her hair. "Orlando is always welcome."

Jude and Gabi wandered off to speak with Quinn and Amelia.

"I need to freshen, uh, check on a few things." Josephine's long elegant fingers fluttered in the air, sending diamonds flashing in the light.

"Would you like me to get everyone settled before we

leave?" Wendy asked Josephine as relatives continued to arrive.

"That would be very much appreciated." Josephine patted her niece's shoulder, even as her gaze remained fixed on the door.

"Everyone." Wendy spoke loudly above the conversational din. "The waiters have appetizers and beverages for you in the party room. The buffet is in the process of being set up. Please make your way down the hall."

"Thank you, dear," Josephine said. "I'm sorry you can't stay."

"Next time," Wendy began.

"Honey, we're late." Marcos took his wife's arm.

After offering Josephine a quick hug, Wendy hurried off with her husband and daughter, stopping for a second where Shannon stood speaking with a couple Oliver didn't recognize. Locals, he decided, noticing the denim and boots.

His mother surprised him by calling Shannon's name and motioning to her when she began to head out the door with Wendy and Marcos. When Shannon sauntered over, Josephine took one of her hands. "I fear I didn't make it clear—I'd love for you to join us."

"C'mon, Shannon, join us. Please." Gabi had returned. She slanted a glance at Oliver. "Shannon made me feel so welcome when I came to stay in Horseback Hollow last year after my father's accident."

Clearly, the two women were friends. Still, Shannon hesitated. "I don't want to intrude."

"You're not intruding." Oliver's gaze locked on hers. "You're very much wanted."

You're very much wanted.
What was there about the sentiment, said in that de-

lightful British accent, that made her want to giggle like a nervous schoolgirl? The words echoed in her head, even as Shannon gestured to Rachel that she'd call her later. Her friend smiled and nodded, then refocused her attention back on the cowboy who was eating the last nacho.

While Ollie remained tightly clutched in his grandmother's arms, Shannon strolled with Oliver down a wide hallway to a large room that resembled the inside of a Mexican hacienda. It had arched doorways, stucco walls of bold red and spicy mustard and a tile floor that complemented the warmth of the walls.

Oliver slanted a sideways glance. "It was fortuitous, running into you here."

"Fortuitous for me." Shannon shot him an impish smile. "I'm getting dinner out of the deal."

"And I will have the pleasure of your company," Oliver said gallantly.

"You're going to be sick of me very soon," she teased with an ease that surprised her. "Underfoot practically 24/7."

"I'll be working a lot of hours," he said seriously. "Our contact will likely be minimal."

Shannon pulled back a scowl. He didn't have to sound so doggone pleased at the prospect. "Hopefully you'll carve out some time to play with Ollie."

Surprise flashed in his eyes. "Entertaining him, keeping him safe and tending to his needs will now be your job."

Before she could formulate a response, she was handed a margarita and Oliver was swept away.

Though Shannon hadn't done much socializing with the British branch of the Fortunes who'd recently arrived in Horseback Hollow, she'd grown up with Jeanne Marie's children. There were seven of them and they were all here tonight, as was Josephine's sister, Jeanne Marie.

Shannon mingled, accepting an empanada appetizer from a passing waiter before taking a seat at a table with Gabi and Kinsley Aaron. Kinsley was the outreach coordinator for the Fortune Foundation and engaged to Christopher Fortune Jones.

Since both women were set to be wed on Valentine's Day, bridal talk dominated the conversation and continued after they went through the buffet line and sat down with their plates of food.

Oliver stood across the room, caught up in conversation with his brother-in-law, Quinn Drummond. Back in middle school, Shannon had the hugest crush on Quinn. When she was thirteen she'd gathered the courage to ask him to a turnabout dance.

When both Quinn and Oliver turned to look at her, Shannon smiled and wiggled her fingers in a semblance of a wave, praying Quinn wasn't relaying to Oliver the awful story of how she'd awkwardly asked him out.

Abruptly she turned to Gabi and bared her teeth as her gaze flickered. "All clear?"

Gabi swallowed a bite of salad. "Perfect. Why?"

"Just checking." Shannon glanced at Gabi's chicken taco salad; heavy on romaine, light on cheese, no tortilla bowl. "How's the salad?"

"Delicious." Gabi smiled. "What about the enchiladas?"

"Truly out of this world." Shannon took another bite, savoring the taste. "You should try one."

The suggestion was out before she remembered Gabi was committed to eating nutritionally. Looking at her, it was hard to believe Gabi had needed a heart transplant when she was nineteen.

"This will fill me up, thanks." Gabi flashed an easy smile and gestured to where Oliver now stood speaking with his sister, Amelia. "Give me your take on Oliver."

Though she and Gabi were currently alone—Kinsley had joined her fiancé at another table—Shannon didn't immediately answer. "What do you mean?"

"You must like him well enough to go to work for him, to live with him."

"I think our *business* arrangement will work out well for both of us." Shannon chose her words carefully, knowing whatever she said stood a good chance of getting back to Oliver.

Jude was his cousin, after all. And Gabi didn't seem the type to have secrets from her fiancé.

"I'm asking what you think of him as a man." Gabi waggled a fork at Shannon. Her dark eyes sparkled. "Admit it. Doesn't that sexy accent make you want to swoon?"

"Who are you swooning over, Gabrielle?" Jude appeared out of nowhere to plop down in the chair Kinsley had recently vacated. "Before you answer, let me warn you that it better be me."

He lifted her hand to his mouth and kissed her knuckles.

"Sorry, Charlie." Gabi wrinkled her nose, her tone teasing. "Your cousin Oliver's accent has us both swooning. Isn't that right, Shannon?"

"That's a kick in the shorts." Though he tried to look stern, Jude failed miserably. Once he got the smile that kept trying to form on his lips under control, he turned and called out, "Oliver, get your ass over here."

Oliver merely glanced over at the sound of his name.

Jude made an impatient "come here" motion with his hand.

After a few final words to his sister, Oliver strode over.

"He was speaking with Amelia." Shannon had a sinking feeling she knew why Jude had summoned Oliver.

"Now he'll be speaking with us," Jude said, suddenly

all affable-cowboy charm. He reached over and pulled up a chair when Oliver approached the table. "Join us."

Oliver's brows pulled together.

Beneath Oliver's polished smile, Shannon saw signs of fatigue. Had everyone forgotten that he'd made a transatlantic flight with a toddler only days earlier?

"What can I do for you, Jude?" Oliver asked.

Shannon thought his eyes may have lingered on her for an extra heartbeat, but she couldn't be certain.

"You can stop making the ladies swoon."

Obviously perplexed, Oliver glanced over at Shannon for clarification.

She simply smiled and shifted her gaze to Jude. This was his bronc in the rodeo, not hers.

"These ladies—" Jude gestured to Shannon and Gabi "—are swooning over your accent."

Oliver ignored Gabi to focus on Shannon. Though she'd never been the wilting-violet, blushing type, heat rose up her neck.

"Actually, it was me." Gabi raised her hand like a schoolgirl eager to talk. "I adore your accent. Though I'm not sure the effect would be the same, can you teach me to speak like you?"

Poor Oliver.

Two lines formed between his brows. It was obvious he didn't quite know what to make of his cousin's soon-to-be bride or the plate of cowboy caviar someone shoved into his hand.

"Gabi's teasing you." Shannon spoke in a matter-of-fact tone and took a sip of the margarita.

"Oh."

"I'm in the mood for some dancing," Jude announced. "Mind keeping the ladies company while I get that started?"

"Dancing?" Shannon smiled. "On what dance floor?"

"That will be remedied momentarily," Jude said over his shoulder.

"Don't even bother trying to figure him out." Gabi's tone was filled with warm affection. The smile was still on her lips when she shifted her attention to Oliver. "I was surprised to see Amelia and Quinn here."

"Why?"

"Their baby is so tiny."

"I'm certain whoever is watching her has been cleared by Scotland Yard."

Oliver sat the plate of "caviar" down just as the sweet melody of a romantic ballad filled the air, followed by Jude's booming voice.

"I don't know about the other grooms-to-be, but with the wedding less than two weeks away, I need to practice my dance steps," Jude said.

"Give it up, Jude," one of his brothers called out. "Practice isn't going to change the fact that you have two left feet."

"He does not," Gabi muttered indignantly.

"Shut up, Chris," Jude shot back good-naturedly. "We're going to use this part of the room for dancin', so everyone put down your drinks and grab a partner."

"That's my man," Gabi said with pride. "A real take-charge guy."

Her take-charge guy returned to the table to pull her to her feet and lead her to the area he had cleared for dancing. They weren't the only couple. All around Shannon and Oliver, men and women were pairing up.

When Shannon saw a woman walk by with a toddler, it struck Shannon that she hadn't seen Ollie for a while. "Where's Ollie?"

"Mum is changing his nappy." Oliver grasped on to

the topic like a drowning man would grab a life jacket. "I couldn't pry him away from her even if I wanted to."

Do you want to, Oliver?

He looked at her so strangely that for a split second Shannon thought she must have spoken aloud. Until she realized his growing unease was because everyone who'd been seated at their table was now dancing.

Oliver pushed back his chair and abruptly stood. When he opened his mouth, Shannon found herself anticipating what it would feel like to be held in his strong arms.

"If you'll excuse me." His head inclined in a slight bow. "I must check on my son."

Oliver turned on his heel and strode off, leaving Shannon alone and, just as when she was thirteen, without a date for the dance.

Chapter Six

By ten the next morning, Oliver had fed his son, changed his nappy for the third time and was ready to get down to business. He placed Ollie in his car seat and set off for the Triple S ranch.

He called Shannon's father to make sure he'd be home, indicating he had something of a personal nature to discuss with him. When Shep had bluntly asked what it was, Oliver told him it was a matter best discussed in person. So here he was, on a bright and sunny Saturday morning in early February, headed over to clarify with a Texas rancher that he didn't have designs on his daughter.

Certainly Shannon intrigued him. How could she not, with eyes the color of rich, dark cocoa and a smile that pierced his reserve as easily as an arrow through marshmallow. Was it any wonder that last night he'd been seriously tempted to ask her to dance?

Oliver wheeled the Mercedes onto the highway, remembering how very close he'd come to asking her. But that, he thought rather righteously, was the difference between a strong man and a weak one. No matter how tempted he was to see what it would feel like to hold her in his arms, Oliver hadn't given in to temptation.

In fact, he'd walked away. Not because he couldn't handle the temptation but because he'd seen the way her foot tapped in time to the music and the longing way she glanced at the couples dancing. By leaving the table, he'd made it easier for other men to ask her.

Yet, when he'd watched his cousin Galen stroll over and Shannon had risen to take his arm, Oliver had felt a twinge of unease. He hoped his cousin was an honorable man.

Oliver couldn't help noticing Galen held her a little too closely when they danced. And why was he whispering in her ear? What could they be saying that was so secretive? It had to be a ploy to get even closer to her. And from what Oliver had observed, it worked.

Actually it was something Oliver might have done if she'd been in his arms. But Shannon was his employee. Not that a man couldn't dance with his employee. But he could never hold her close.

The last thing Oliver wanted was to mess up a good working relationship before it even began. Some women could handle a casual, meaningless affair. He had the distinct impression that Shannon wasn't like those women. In fact, she'd made it clear she wanted a business relationship only. He'd agreed. He'd given her his word. And a gentleman always kept his word.

Though right now Oliver didn't feel much like a gentleman.

Thoughts of Shannon occupied him during the rest of the drive to the Singleton ranch. By the time Oliver turned onto the long lane leading to the house, Ollie was fast asleep. Oliver stifled a groan at the sight of the boy's lolling head in the rearview mirror. He'd discovered if Ollie napped throughout the day, he often didn't sleep well at night.

But Oliver couldn't concern himself with that now. He would get through another night of little to no sleep with the thought that tomorrow night Shannon would be there to take care of Ollie. And Oliver would finally be able to get back to business.

For now, he had a different kind of business to attend to, and he wasn't looking forward to it.

Before confirming a time, he'd asked Shep if Shannon was home. According to Shep, she'd left early that morning to attend a "farmers' market" in Vicker's Corners and wasn't expected back until noon. By that time, Oliver's business should be concluded.

The Singleton home was a two-story with white siding, black shutters and a wraparound porch. The bushes on each side of the walk leading to the front steps looked like a sturdy variety with burnished red leaves and tiny thorns.

Oliver noticed the ceiling of the porch was painted blue, like the sky. Seeing the swing made him wonder if Shannon ever sat there and shared kisses with some lucky man while a full moon shone overhead.

Oliver chuckled at the fanciful thought and shifted Ollie's weight in his arms. Though his son was by no means fat, he was sturdy, weighing in at approximately a stone and a half. Not that easy to carry when he squirmed as he was doing now.

Having Ollie with him wasn't ideal but Oliver had brought some of the boy's favorite toys, so hopefully that would keep him occupied during the brief discussion with Shannon's father.

When Oliver reached the front door, he had Ollie stand beside him while he rang the bell.

The door opened several seconds later.

"You must be Oliver." Shep Singleton was a tall man in his late fifties with a thick thatch of gray hair and a lean, weathered face.

Dressing down for the occasion had been a smart move, Oliver decided. Though he considered this a business call, he hadn't worn his suit. Instead he'd taken a page from Jensen's playbook and chosen a pair of khakis and a polo.

Even with the concession, he felt overdressed compared with Shep's jeans and flannel shirt.

Because Shep didn't extend his hand, Oliver kept his own at his side.

"Come in." Shep motioned to him. "Lilian has coffee brewin' and she's cutting some slices of her blue-ribbon banana bread."

Oliver didn't think he'd ever had blue-ribbon banana bread. In fact he was fairly certain he'd never had regular banana bread. He considered asking how blue ribbon differed from regular, just for his own edification, but decided it wasn't important. Not when they had more important things to discuss.

He followed Shep into a foyer that was pleasant but unremarkable, with a staircase straight ahead and a parlor to the right. Because the older man's strides were long, Oliver was forced to pick up Ollie to keep pace.

The kitchen was as old-fashioned as the rest of the house, with appliances the color of avocado and a chrome kitchen table with a swirly gray-green top. There was an ornamental print on the wall with teapots and kettles of all shapes and colors.

A slender woman who reminded Oliver of her daughter, with warm brown eyes and hair the color of strong tea, turned to greet him.

"It's so good to finally meet you," Lilian said with a warm, welcoming smile. "When Shep told me you were stopping by, I hoped you'd be bringing this little guy with you."

Her gaze lingered on Ollie, and a soft look filled her eyes. She reached inside a clown jar and pulled out what looked like an oat biscuit. The questioning look in her eyes had Oliver nodding.

Lilian moved slowly to the child, who stood looking around the colorful kitchen with a wide, unblinking look of wonder.

"Hi, Ollie." She crouched down with the ease of a woman used to constant movement.

The toddler stared at her.

"Do you like cookies?" Lilian held it up in front of him, and when she was certain she had his attention, she broke off a piece and held it out to him.

A shy smile hovered on Ollie's lips. Still, after a moment, he reached out and took the piece from her hand, shoving it into his mouth.

"Ollie, what do you say to Mrs. Singleton?" Oliver prompted.

"Tank ooh," Ollie spoke around a mouthful of cookie.

Lilian ruffled his hair in a casual gesture and stood. "He's darling. Shannon has four younger brothers, so we're used to boys around this house."

"Four boys." Oliver almost cringed. He had a difficult time managing one. "That must have kept you busy."

"I'll say. For years I didn't know if I was coming or going. I longed for just a couple hours to myself. Even fifteen minutes." She laughed and a wistful look crossed her face. "Now I'd give anything to have that time back."

Her gaze dropped to Ollie. "Cherish every minute with your son. Time goes by so quickly."

Shep cleared his throat. "I told Oliver you had some banana bread for us. And coffee."

Lilian flashed a smile. "What's conversation without coffee and banana bread?"

Without realizing how it happened, Oliver was at the table with a steaming mug of strong coffee before him and a small plate containing delicious-smelling bread still warm from the oven.

He waited for Lilian to dispense the sterling, but when none was forthcoming and he saw Shep pick up the slice and take a bite, Oliver followed suit. When in Rome...

"This blue-ribbon banana bread is excellent," he told Lilian, making her blush.

"Last year it won a purple at the state fair."

Oliver simply nodded and smiled. He made a mental note to ask his sister about a "purple."

"Well, I'll leave you boys to your business." Lilian refilled their coffee cups before her gaze shifted to Oliver. "Being as it's such a nice day, I thought I'd air out some blankets on the line. Would you mind if I took Ollie with me? I promise I'll keep an eye on him."

Oliver hesitated. "He's wanted to stay close lately. Last night he didn't even want my mum to hold him."

Of course, his mother had unthinkingly swooped in, startling him. Still, Ollie had recently become cautious around people he didn't know. Other than Shannon. He'd taken to her right off.

"Do you mind if I give it a try?"

"Not at all." It would be easier to speak with Shep if he didn't have to keep Ollie occupied.

"Ollie." Lilian crouched down beside the boy, who still

held the scruffy yellow tiger he'd had when Oliver had picked him up from Diane's parents.

According to Diane's mum, they'd given the stuffed animal to Ollie when he was born, and it was a favorite of his. She'd had tears in her eyes when she'd relayed the story, Oliver recalled.

At the time, Oliver hadn't paid much mind to her. He'd been so angry with them for withholding information of Diane's death. For keeping his son from him.

"Would you like to go outside with me? You can take Mr. Tiger with you, if you like," her voice continued, low, calm and soothing.

There was something about the way Lilian spoke that reminded Oliver of Shannon. An intonation. Or a certain cadence in her speech. Not an accent, though the woman certainly sounded American. He finally concluded it was the warmth that wove through each word like a wool scarf on a foggy morning.

Whatever the reason, Ollie responded the same way to Lilian as he had to Shannon. Instantly and with no hesitation.

Lilian took his hand in hers. The two made it all the way to the door leading outside before they turned back. "Say, 'Bye-bye, Daddy. See you soon.'"

She demonstrated a wave for the child.

"Bye-bye," Ollie said in his high-pitched, sweet baby voice. "See you soon."

Oliver smiled, even though he noticed Ollie didn't call him "Daddy." He never did. Of course his vocabulary was rather limited, consisting of only twenty-five words. Still, if Ollie could say the dog's name, shouldn't he be able to say "Daddy"?

Once the back door banged shut, Oliver decided to get

right to the point. "I suppose you're wondering why I'm here."

Shep lifted his piece of bread. "I figure you're fixin' to tell me."

The older man bit into the bread, then washed the piece down with a swig of coffee. He leaned back in his chair and studied Oliver intently.

For a second Oliver felt like one of those young lads in films, meeting his girl's parents for the first time. Oliver had no personal experience in this arena. He'd been sent to a preparatory school when he was thirteen. Functions with suitable girls' schools had been prearranged. No parents involved.

"Your daughter has agreed to be Ollie's nanny while I'm in Horseback Hollow."

"She mentioned something about that the other night," Shep admitted.

Oliver felt a surprising surge of relief. "Then you don't have a problem with her moving in."

The mug of coffee Shep had lifted to his mouth froze in midair. He lowered it slowly until it came to rest on the table.

Unlike his daughter's, Shep's eyes were a piercing pale blue. Oliver felt the full force of his gaze punch into him.

"Move in. With you?"

"Not with me," Oliver clarified, keeping his tone conversational. "Into the house."

"Your house."

"Technically your house," Oliver pointed out.

"Don't give me any double-talk, boy." Shep's eyes narrowed and Oliver felt as if he were in the crosshairs of his father's foul temper once again.

Though Rhys Henry Hayes hadn't remained married to Josephine for long, it had been long enough for them to have two sons together, and for his father to make Oliver's life a living hell.

"Shannon will always be treated with respect when she's under my roof." Oliver met Shep's gaze with a calm one of his own.

As a young boy, Oliver had vowed he'd never be intimidated by any man ever again. "That's why I'm here. To let you know she will be my son's nanny. My employee. Nothing more. She's safe with me."

Shep's expression gave nothing away. He took a big gulp of coffee before he responded. "Shannon is twenty-five. As much as I'd like to, I can't make her decisions. But I will speak bluntly."

"Please do," Oliver said quietly.

"After what happened in Lubbock, after that incident, I don't feel comfortable with her being there with only a baby in diapers as a chaperone."

Oliver cocked his head. "What incident in Lubbock?"

"Oliver."

Shannon paused in the doorway, taking in the cozy scene with her father and Oliver at the table. She let her gaze sweep over the half-eaten pieces of banana bread and coffee mugs in need of refills.

"Your father was about to tell me about some incident in Lubbock," Oliver told her.

Despite telling herself not to react, Shannon felt her spine grow rigid, vertebra by vertebra. She shot her father a fulminating glance that, as usual, he ignored.

"Correct me if I'm wrong, but I believe that's my story to tell. Or not." Forcing a smile, Shannon shifted her attention back to Oliver. "It's not all that interesting. I had a boss who got a little handsy. It's over and done. I've moved on."

The back door clattered and seconds later, her mother

strode into the room, Ollie chattering happily at her side. "Shannon, honey. When did you get home?"

"Just walked through the door," Shannon answered absently, her mind back in Lubbock. She didn't like thinking of that time. It was in the past and she meant what she'd said to Oliver—she'd moved on. "Do you have any more banana bread?"

"It'll spoil your appetite for lunch," her father warned.

Some things never change, Shannon thought ruefully. But instead of being irritated, she found the knowledge strangely reassuring.

"You're eating it," she pointed out. "Won't it spoil *your* lunch?"

"Nope." Shep grinned and popped the last bite into his mouth.

Shannon rolled her eyes. "Oh, honestly."

Oliver's gaze traveled between her and her father, as if he found their simple exchange fascinating.

Out of the corner of her eye, Shannon saw Ollie run across the room to Oliver. He swung the child onto his lap with a welcoming smile.

Shannon's heart swelled. How could she have ever thought this man didn't care about his son?

"I hope the bread didn't spoil your appetite, Oliver. I'd love to have you join us for lunch." Lilian wrapped the rest of the loaf in plastic wrap. "We're having quiche."

Shep grimaced. "Aw, Lil, why not burgers?"

"Too much red meat isn't good for you." Lilian's argument was an old one, repeated daily. She shifted to Oliver. "We're also having a nice salad of dark greens with a balsamic vinaigrette I make myself."

"What happened to the good ole days of iceberg and Thousand Island?" Shep groused.

Lilian ignored the comment to focus on their guest. "If

you don't think Ollie would like quiche, I can rustle him
up some mac and cheese."

Shannon expected Oliver to make some excuse to leave.
Once again he surprised her.

"Thank you, Mrs. Singleton." He gestured to the now-
empty plate before him. "If your quiche is as good as your
blue-ribbon banana bread, I'm in for a treat."

"Splendid. And please, call me Lilian." Her mother
smiled. "If you and Shep have concluded your conversation, why don't you take Shannon and Ollie out to the
porch and check out the swing? It's a beautiful day and
it'll give me a chance to clear the table and get ready for
lunch. Shouldn't be more than a half hour or so."

Oliver rose and smiled at Shannon. "I don't know that
I've ever sat with a pretty woman on a porch swing before."

Shep shoved back his chair. "I'll join you."

"Honey." Lilian covered the sharp tone with a laugh.
"You're not going anywhere. You're staying right here and
helping me."

"I can help you, Mother."

"No, no. Your father will help." Lilian turned to her
husband and looped her arm through his. "Shep, sweetie,
I think I may have a bottle of Thousand Island in the pan-
try after all. Why don't you look for it while Shannon and
Oliver head outside?"

Shannon thought about telling her mother she knew exactly where to find the salad dressing, but kept her mouth
shut. Her mother had it in her head that she and Oliver were
going to have some time alone on the swing, and there was
no getting around that.

Besides, Shannon was curious about what Oliver and
her father had been discussing when she arrived. For that
matter, she wanted to know exactly what had brought Oliver to the Singleton ranch this morning in the first place.

At this moment, she hadn't a clue. Oliver was a difficult man to figure out. Like last night at the dinner party. They'd been having a perfectly lovely conversation when he'd ditched her. Once he'd left the table, she hadn't seen him again all evening.

She'd enjoyed a couple of dances with his cousin, then headed out. Now she arrived home to find him shooting the breeze with her dad.

"Oliver." She looped her arm through his and shot him the same sugary-sweet smile her mother had offered her father only seconds earlier. "Let's swing and you can tell me what brought you all the way out here this morning."

Chapter Seven

Though it was only February, the outside temperature felt more like June. Thankfully there was a light breeze from the north and the covered porch shielded Oliver and Shannon from the worst of the midday sun. Shannon took a seat at one end of the swing and Oliver sat down with Ollie at the other.

Almost immediately, the child left his father's lap to scoot over to Shannon. He rested his head on her lap and she automatically began to stroke his soft brown hair. In seconds, his eyelids closed and he fell quickly asleep.

"He shouldn't be that tired." Oliver glanced down at his son with a worried frown. "He slept in the car on the way here."

"Little boys expend a lot of energy." Shannon smiled, then sobered as she remembered there was something they needed to discuss. She met his gaze. "Tell me why you came all the way out here today."

"To speak with your father."

Shannon curbed her impatience and merely lifted a brow. "About?"

"The comments Marcos made last night got me to thinking." Oliver shifted on the white lacquered slats. "I decided to reassure your father you would be safe and respected under my roof."

Shannon pressed her lips together and counted to five. "I am in charge of my own life, Oliver. Whatever goes on, or doesn't, under your roof is our business. Not my father's. Not my mother's. Understand?"

He stared at her for a long moment. "I see your point."

"I appreciate that your intentions came from a good place," she acknowledged. "But this is between us."

She wasn't sure exactly what all "this" encompassed, but for now it was simply the job and taking care of Ollie.

"You went behind my back." Shannon did her best to keep the hurt from her voice. After growing up in a family of men, she'd learned there was no quicker turnoff than to lead from emotion. "You never even mentioned you were considering speaking with my father."

"That's because it was something I decided last night."

"There were opportunities during the evening when you could have discussed your concerns with me," she said pointedly.

He reluctantly nodded, then surprised them both by reaching over and taking her hand. "Apologies. I overstepped."

She searched his gaze and saw only sincerity.

"Accepted." Shannon made no move to pull her hand away as the swing moved slowly.

"What happened in Lubbock?"

She blinked and jerked her fingers free. "I already told you."

"You said your previous employer got 'handsy.' That's not much of an explanation."

Should she tell him? If so, how much should she say? Even though it wasn't all that long ago, in Shannon's mind it was ancient history. She'd moved on. Still, it wasn't as if she had anything to hide, and if she didn't spill, she wouldn't put it past Oliver to do some investigating on his own.

"My last job was with a marketing firm in Lubbock. My direct supervisor, Jerry, was the CEO's nephew." Though Shannon did her best to keep her voice matter-of-fact, it shook slightly. She continued to stroke Ollie's hair and found the motion relaxed her. "He wasn't much older than me, but he was married with two kids."

Oliver made an encouraging sound.

Shannon felt the urge to get up and pace, but couldn't because of Ollie. The twist in her belly told her she wasn't completely over what had happened. Not fully, anyway.

"Jerry seemed nice at first, though there was something about him that put me on alert. Too many compliments of a personal nature, and whenever he was at my desk, he stood too close. I told myself I was just overreacting. At my previous job I'd worked with all women, so overreacting seemed plausible."

Oliver didn't speak, simply inclined his head in a gesture that seemed to indicate she should keep talking.

"Then he started touching me."

Oliver's head jerked up and a muscle in his jaw jumped. "Touching you?"

"It started out innocent enough—a hand on my shoulder while he leaned over to look at my computer screen, brushing back a strand of hair from my face." Shannon gazed down at Ollie's head resting in her lap. She swallowed past the dryness in her throat. "I told him the touching made me uncomfortable. But no matter what I said, he turned it around and made me wonder if I was being too sensitive. You know, making something out of nothing."

"He made you doubt your instincts."

"Yes. He didn't listen to my concerns, didn't acknowledge they were valid. I let the issue drop. That was my first mistake."

"What happened?" Oliver asked in a low, tight voice.

"One night, shortly before Thanksgiving, we were working late. I made a point to never be alone with him. It started out as four of us working on a campaign. The other two ended up leaving. I was almost finished so I stayed behind. That was my second mistake."

Without her quite realizing how it had happened, her hand was once again in Oliver's. The warmth of his strong fingers wrapping around hers gave Shannon the strength to continue.

"He—he pulled me to him, kissed me, told me his wife and kids were out of town and we'd have his house to ourselves. No one would ever know." Shame bubbled up inside Shannon. "He wouldn't let go of me. Finally I was able to jerk away. My shirt tore. I started crying."

"Bastard," she thought she heard Oliver mutter.

"I reminded him he was a married man. He laughed and called me a tease. But when I said I was going to his boss, he turned the tables again and accused me of coming on to him. Said he was shocked and appalled by my behavior. Then he asked who did I think his uncle would believe? Him, an upstanding family man and deacon of his church? Or me? A single woman who'd never complained about his behavior until now?" Shannon lifted her gaze to meet Oliver's. "I turned in my resignation without even giving notice. I returned to Horseback Hollow and put it all behind me."

Oliver's fingers tightened around hers.

She waited for him to say that she should have stood up for herself, should have at least told his uncle the story, but to her relief he didn't.

"I loved my job," she added. "It was hard to walk away. But I didn't see that I had any choice."

"You made the best decision for you."

"I did." Shannon felt herself relax and was sorry when Oliver released her hand. "Though it still makes me angry you went behind my back, it's probably a good thing you spoke with my father. He doesn't have a very high opinion of male employers right now."

"I meant what I said," Oliver told her. "You're perfectly safe with me."

Shannon could only wonder why she found his words more disappointing than reassuring.

When Oliver arrived home later, it was after two. By then Ollie was cranky and out of sorts. After changing his nappy, Oliver sat the boy down on the rug in the living room with his bricks, hoping a little quiet play would relax him.

But Ollie refused to be distracted or comforted. He knocked down the stack that Oliver had arranged, then picked up one and flung it across the room. When Oliver tried to put him down for a nap, he stood at the edge of the playpen and cried, rocking back and forth like a monkey in a cage as tears slipped down his chubby cheeks.

Though Oliver had some catching up to do on market indices, he lifted his son up and settled into the rocker with him. Every time Ollie pulled back, Oliver would bring him back against him. Finally the boy quit struggling, his hands resting on his shoulders as Oliver rocked him. Back and forth. Back and forth.

Oliver wondered if Diane had ever rocked Ollie. Or, for that matter, had Mrs. Crowder, his London nanny? This was a first for him, but he'd been desperate. As he felt his son relax against him, Oliver realized rocking was really quite nice. A connection. Between him and Ollie.

A connection that only served to remind him how much of Ollie's life he'd missed.

Not insisting on regular visitation had been a mistake. Just as Shannon not pressing charges against her boss had been a mistake. In his estimation the man shouldn't be able to harass an employee—hell, *assault* an employee—and get away with it.

Not only get away with it, but make her feel as if the whole thing was somehow her fault. That's why he hadn't added to her guilt by suggesting she could have handled the situation differently. She'd made the best decision based on where she was at the time.

Oliver closed his eyes, realizing he was more tired than he thought. Adjusting to a different time zone while having total care of a small boy had proved more difficult than he'd initially envisioned.

His respect for mothers and nannies had gone up a thousandfold...

Oliver awoke to a small hand pressed against his face. When his lids eased open, he found himself staring directly into Ollie's bright eyes.

"Up," Ollie ordered. "Get up."

The child could say "get up" but couldn't manage "Daddy"?

By the foul smell permeating the air, Oliver knew Ollie wouldn't simply need a nappy change. He'd probably need a bath, as well. His prediction proved correct.

It wasn't until Ollie was changed, bathed and fed that it struck Oliver that the child's schedule was going to be disrupted once again. Tonight was Amelia and Quinn's baby shower. He wasn't certain what to expect, but he assumed a gift was de rigueur. Thankfully, Oliver hadn't had a chance to give them the limited-edition Highgrove baby hamper he'd picked up at Harrods department store before he left London.

Though he wasn't sure if Amelia was still into organic supplies or not, the hamper contained not only a fully jointed antique mohair Highgrove bear, but an assortment of organic baby products created with a blend of oils to be calm and soothing to a baby's skin. The salesclerk had assured him the baby hamper was a popular gift for new mothers.

Diane had been a new mother once. Had she been as thrilled by Ollie as Amelia was by Clementine? Perhaps.

Oliver raked a hand through his hair. Their marriage had already been in trouble when Ollie was born. He'd dealt with the increased tension and Diane's unhappiness in the only way he knew how, by working even harder and giving her expensive trinkets. It hadn't been enough. Oliver expelled a heavy push of air, feeling the full weight of his failure.

He placed Ollie in the Pack 'n Play and watched his son pick up a toy truck with a squeal of delight.

He'd made so many mistakes...

Banishing the unproductive thoughts and emotions, Oliver motioned Barnaby off the sofa and headed for the shower. He'd never been to a couple's baby party. Gabi and Jude were hosting the event, held at his aunt Jeanne Marie's spacious ranch home.

By the time Oliver arrived, cars and trucks lined both sides of the graveled drive. He parked at the end of the long line. A truck immediately pulled in behind him.

He paid little attention, his focus on releasing Ollie from

his car seat. They were late and Oliver prided himself on being punctual. However, when he'd let Barnaby outside, right before they were to leave home, the dog had run off. Oliver had wasted precious minutes looking for the animal, who'd received a stern lecture once he returned.

"We're going to have to quit meeting like this."

He turned and there was Shannon, wearing a shirt and skirt the color of mint, her hair pulled back in a casual twist.

"You look amazing," he said.

"You don't look so bad yourself." Her gaze settled momentarily on his gray trousers and open-necked white shirt. "Let me hold your gift while you fumble with the car seat."

"Fumble is right." Oliver gave a laugh. "He's strapped in tighter than most astronauts."

Shannon stood close while he unbuckled Ollie. The light vanilla scent of her perfume was pleasing. "I should have realized you'd be here, what with Amelia being your sister."

"A sister who is a bugger about punctuality."

"We're not that—" Shannon glanced at her watch. "Eek. You're right. We are late. We need to hoof it."

She started down the lane toward the house at a surprisingly fast clip, the gifts hugged to her chest.

Oliver scooped up Ollie and headed after her.

They reached the house at the same time and climbed the steps to the porch in unison. Oliver rang the bell.

It was only seconds before the door opened and Jude waved them inside.

The gifts were lifted from Shannon's hands and Gabi directed Oliver to a temporary playroom set up at the back of the house. Several children were already there, along with two teenage child-care workers.

To Oliver's surprise, Ollie screeched in excitement and hurried over to pick up a plastic bat. Oliver only shook his head. His son's mercurial moods were a constant mystery. He told the teenage babysitter to come and get him if Ollie got scared.

As he didn't want to simply disappear—though the thought was tempting—Oliver walked over to Ollie and told him he was leaving and would be back soon. Ollie blinked, opening and closing his hand in the gesture Lilian had taught him. "Bye-bye."

Before leaving the room, Oliver reiterated to the young woman monitoring the door not to hesitate to retrieve him if Ollie turned fussy. He saw by the look on her face she'd written him off as just another overprotective parent. Especially considering Ollie was now happily banging the plastic bat like a drum on the floor.

His duty completed, Oliver hurried from the room and found Shannon waiting with two flutes of champagne. She shoved one into his hand. "For you."

"Thank you." He took a sip and found the vintage very much to his taste. As they strolled down the hall, Oliver began to relax. "This evening may not be so bad after all."

"I'll ask how you feel after the games."

"Games?"

"Oh, yeah," Shannon said as they headed into the large double parlor where the guests were congregated. "You can't have a baby shower without games."

Oliver couldn't begin to imagine what kind of games she meant.

"There's the last couple," Gabi called out when he and Shannon entered the parlor. "We can get started now."

For a second, Oliver looked around to see whom she meant until he realized she was talking about him and

Shannon. He started to protest until he saw Shannon's friend Rachel had been paired with Quinn's elderly aunt.

Not that he minded being paired with Shannon for whatever games they would play; he simply didn't want to put her in an awkward position of everyone thinking they were a couple.

"What's the game, Gabi?" Shannon smiled easily, looking relaxed among this group of friends.

Even though Amelia was his sister and he was family, Oliver was clearly the outsider today. Though he was proficient at social conversation, he was rather relieved Gabi appeared ready to launch into the scheduled activities.

The first game was a baby word scramble. Each "team" was given twenty words where the letters had been scrambled. Oliver was, by nature, a competitive person. He quickly discovered Shannon shared his must-win attitude.

Sitting beside each other on an overstuffed sofa, they breezed through the first nineteen words. Then they reached number twenty.

"BELOTT." Shannon gazed down at the word. Her brows pulled together.

Oliver knew he should be studying the letters. But the simple task of focusing had become increasingly difficult with each word. He couldn't take his eyes off the side of Shannon's face, off the graceful arch of her neck, off the woman who took his breath away.

Her choice of attire for the evening only made it more difficult for him to concentrate. The shirt she wore was a thin fabric. If Oliver looked hard enough, he could practically see right through it to the smooth expanse of creamy skin and the lacy...

His mouth went dry.

"We've got eighteen," he heard Quinn's aunt announce to the room. "Two more and we win."

"One left," Amber said to Jensen.

Shannon leaned closer, as if she thought practically having her nose on the paper would unscramble the word.

All the closeness actually did was further scramble his brain until he couldn't think of anything but how good she smelled and wonder how good she'd taste.

"Twenty," Christopher called in triumph and high-fived Kinsley, then kissed her thoroughly to cheers and applause.

"The last one was the easiest," Kinsley said when she came up for air.

Oliver exchanged a glance with Shannon. She lifted her shoulders in a wordless gesture.

"What was it?" Oliver whispered.

"I have no idea," she said, her tone low and for his ears only. "But I'll find out."

"I'll pick up everyone's papers." Shannon jumped to her feet, collecting the paper and pencils.

She returned to Oliver's side seconds later. "You'll never guess."

He leaned close. "Tell me."

"Bottle."

He groaned. "How did we miss that one?"

"The question is how could we decipher *diaper genie* and fall apart on *bottle*." She laughed good-naturedly. "I guess you can't win 'em all."

As the evening progressed, Shannon discovered Oliver always played to win, whether it was "pin the diaper on the baby" or making a "baby" out of Play-Doh.

But all the Fortunes were competitive. It wasn't until they announced who'd guessed closest to the number of candies in the three-foot-high baby bottle that Oliver claimed his first victory.

"We did it, Shannon." His wide grin made him look years younger.

Actually, he'd done it. She'd wanted to go lower, but he'd convinced her to put the higher number on the guess.

By the time they got to cake and gifts, Shannon had almost forgotten this was a baby shower, an event she normally avoided like the plague. Mainly because it always reminded her she was still alone with no one special in her life.

Oliver stood across the room visiting with his sister when the babysitter appeared in the doorway holding Ollie's hand. The boy's face was tear-streaked. Drops of moisture glistened on his dark lashes.

"He wants his mom and dad," the girl announced to no one in particular.

"I'll take him." Shannon held out her arms and Ollie lunged toward her. She hefted him up and settled him on her hip. "Hey, bud, what's got you so upset?"

Ollie's only answer was to press his face into her neck.

"Looks like he's already halfway in love with you."

Shannon's heart gave a leap but her expression was nonchalant as she turned toward Rachel. "To whom are you referring?"

"Little Ollie. The kid has you in a death grip." Rachel leaned around Shannon and smiled at the boy. "Hi, Ollie. Remember me?"

Ollie burrowed deeper against Shannon.

"I guess I can't impress all the men." Rachel straightened and gave a little laugh. "By the way, it's totally not fair I ended up with Quinn's auntie and you got Oliver."

Shannon smiled benignly. "You've always told me life isn't fair."

Rachel thought for a second then grinned. "You're right.

I'm going to snag one of the leftover baby bottles. Want one?"

Shannon shook her head. The game where the goal was to finish a baby bottle filled with beer had been incredibly frustrating. Who knew bottles emptied so slowly? "No thanks. I've got my hands full right now."

"Later, gator." Rachel gave Ollie a cheeky grin then strolled off.

"Gator." Ollie lifted his head. "Gator."

"That's good, Ollie." Shannon thought for a second. "Can you say...Shannon?"

He stared at her. For a second his oh-so-serious expression reminded her of Oliver. Then he smiled and her heart melted. "Mama."

Shannon chuckled. "Sha-non."

"Mama," he repeated, flinging his arms around her neck.

Though it made absolutely no sense, tears stung the backs of her eyes and she hugged Ollie extra tight. He was so young to be without a mother.

"Amelia is ready to cut the cake." Oliver paused, appearing to notice Ollie for the first time. "What happened?"

"He wanted his daddy." Shannon continued to rub the child's back. "You were busy so we've been bonding. And he's fine now. Aren't you, bud?"

She tickled his ribs and the toddler giggled.

Oliver smiled. "He's pretty heavy. I can take him."

"He's fine." Shannon cuddled Ollie. "Amelia and Quinn sure received a lot of nice gifts for Clementine."

"They did," Oliver agreed, rocking back on the heels of his Ferragamo shoes.

She'd enjoyed watching Oliver mingle with his family in such a relaxed atmosphere. This was why he was in Horseback Hollow. To get reacquainted. To spend time with his sister and his new niece.

"I can tend to Ollie while you socialize." If she could take some of the pressure off him by watching Ollie tonight, she was happy to do it.

"I'm content where I am at the moment," he told her. "Except, I fancy a cake. And some ice cream. Shall I get some for both of us?"

"A man who knows the way to my heart," she teased.

His slow smile had said heart doing flip-flops.

"I'll take that as a yes." Oliver shot her a wink and everything inside her went gooey. "Be right back."

Shannon watched him cross the room to the refreshment table and realized in only a few short days, Oliver Fortune Hayes's happiness had become important to her.

The question was...why?

The reason, she decided, when he reappeared with a slice of strawberry cake in one hand and chocolate in the other, was one best pondered on a full stomach.

Chapter Eight

Spending his Sunday evening grocery shopping at the Superette was not the way Oliver envisioned ending his weekend. Especially after a baby shower had disrupted his normal activities last night.

Oh, whom was he kidding? Nothing had been normal since the day he arrived in Horseback Hollow. But he'd been hopeful that had been about to change. He'd planned on spending the evening preparing for his first full day of work since arriving in Texas. Then Shannon had brought up the serious lack of food in the house.

"What do you think about an asparagus and goat cheese frittata for dinner?" Shannon stopped in front of the dairy case. "I have a great recipe."

"If you're certain it's no trouble."

"No trouble at all." Shannon flashed him a smile. "I love to cook."

She placed a carton of eggs in the shopping trolley, an odd-looking contraption that resembled a red race car.

Though Ollie was strapped in, the boy didn't seem to mind. He happily turned the steering wheel in front of him.

As they went up and down the aisles picking out fruits and vegetables, bread and crackers, Oliver realized he and Diane had never gone to the grocery shop together. He wasn't certain she'd ever gone herself. She may have simply had one of the help handle the mundane task. Perhaps she'd called in the order.

Though Oliver wouldn't exactly call the excursion fun, it wasn't altogether tedious. In almost every aisle they'd run across one of his relatives or a friend of Shannon's. They'd talk for several minutes before continuing down the aisle. Then they'd run into someone else and another conversation would ensue.

The "quick" trip to the store was turning into quite an affair. Still, by the number of groceries in the basket, Shannon had been correct in her assessment. They had been seriously short on rations.

The truth was, he'd spent so much time making sure her room was ready that he'd given little thought to the food situation.

"Does Ollie like these organic food purees?"

Oliver stared at the two pouches she held up, one marked Sweet Potato and the other Blueberry. Had Ollie ever had these? Did he like them? Shannon might as well have asked him to name the ingredients in "blue-ribbon banana bread." "No clue."

Shannon tossed them into the buggy. "I have a friend in Lubbock with a little girl about Ollie's age. Her daughter loves them, so we'll take a chance. They're really good for a growing child."

He bowed to her wisdom. As the oldest of five and with friends who had children, she had the experience and knowledge he needed. Yet, it seemed he should know what food his son preferred.

By the time they reached the checkout lane, the trolley was full. He waited for the cashier to call for someone to assist her. But when Shannon began to drop items into the sacks once they were scanned, Oliver stepped up.

"You picked out the food," he told her. "I'll place them into the sacks."

Ignoring her dubious look, he attacked the task with gusto. His logical mind concluded heavier items should go at the bottom and he shouldn't place cleaning supplies next to food items. Shannon offered additional tips as she sorted the groceries into groups.

"I was a sacker in high school," she said when he gaped at her quick hands.

"You held a position while you were in school?" He paused, nonplussed, a bag of organic apples in his hand.

"Of course." She distracted a whining Ollie by having his stuffed tiger zoom toward him like an airplane. "When there are five kids in your family, if you want something extra you have to work for it."

Oliver simply nodded, though he couldn't relate at all to that logic. In his family there were six children. He and his brother Brodie were from his mother's first marriage. There were four children, his half siblings, from her second marriage to Sir Simon Chesterfield. Oliver felt confident all had received the same admonition growing up: excelling in the classroom was the only priority.

Once the groceries were stowed, he pointed the rental car toward home. As had become his pattern, Ollie fell asleep in his car seat. And when Oliver pulled into the driveway of the ranch house, Ollie woke up, all smiles and full of energy.

Oliver rounded the car to open Shannon's door, but she

was already out of the vehicle and releasing Ollie from his car seat. She helped the boy climb down, then turned to help Oliver with the groceries.

He held up a hand when she reached for a sack. "I will bring these inside. You can put them wherever you like in the cabinets."

"Okay." Despite her agreement, she snatched a small bag of produce. "I'll take this one in with me. That way you'll have one less bag to carry. Oh, and don't worry about Barnaby. Ollie and I will let him out."

With a sassy toss of her head, she strode to the door with Ollie on her hip and a sack of produce in her arms. She had a terrific figure. The way the denim hugged her backside brought a stab of heat and a plethora of lascivious thoughts.

Belatedly reminding himself that the woman he was lusting after was his employee, Oliver forced his gaze from her derriere and back to the groceries in the boot. By the time he'd brought all of the sacks inside and Shannon had put the food away, they were all hungry.

While Shannon whipped up the frittata, he put Ollie in the high chair and fed him leftover chicken from lunch, apples and a pureed pouch of sweet potatoes.

The boy ate with a single-minded determination Oliver couldn't help but admire. Though the cook had tended to Ollie's culinary needs back in London, Oliver found he enjoyed watching his son dive into the food and learning what he liked…and didn't like.

When Ollie finished eating, the sun had set and the serviceable kitchen took on a warm, pleasant glow. The unexpected sound of rain pattering on the roof only added to the ambiance.

"Looks like we arrived home just in time." Oliver pushed back the curtains. Rain fell in sheets and when the thunder boomed, Barnaby left Ollie's side to dive under the table.

Shannon moved to where Oliver stood and gazed out. The arousing scent of vanilla teased Oliver's nostrils. He wanted nothing more than to see if she tasted as good as she smelled. But if his nearness had a similar effect on her, it didn't show.

She stepped back and turned toward the stove. "I love the sound of rain on a roof."

I love being with you.

Considering that he'd already acknowledged enjoying her company, the sentiment shouldn't have surprised him, but it did.

The frittata, accompanied by a green salad, was soon on the table. Oliver brought out a bottle of Chablis, and once he'd poured them each a glass, he held his up in a toast. "To an enjoyable working relationship."

Her glass clinked against his. She smiled. When she took a sip, he felt a hard punch of awareness. Heat simmered in the air, and once their eyes locked he couldn't look away.

Shannon's eyes darkened until they looked almost black in the light. A splash of pink colored both her cheeks. When she moistened her lips with the tip of her tongue, Oliver nearly groaned in agony.

He wanted her. In his bed. On the floor. Heck, the kitchen table would do quite nicely in a pinch.

He wanted to strip off her clothes, touch her...

"Oliver."

Through his haze of desire, he became aware that she was speaking to him.

"Uh, yes?" His gaze remained focused on her lips, as full and lush as a ripe strawberry. He had no doubt she would taste just as sweet.

"I brought some snickerdoodle cookies with me. My mom and I made them earlier today. Would you like one for dessert?"

His foggy brain fought to process the words. Snickerdoodle? Had she really just asked if he wanted a cookie?

He opened his mouth to say he wanted *her*, not some damned biscuit, but instead found himself nodding.

"You won't be sorry." A pleased smile lifted those delectable lips. "They're delicious."

Oliver was already sorry. Sorry he had to settle for a biscuit instead of what he really wanted for dessert tonight.

After dinner, Oliver surprised Shannon by offering to clean up the kitchen so she could get settled. She immediately accepted the offer. Happy to have the time to get settled, Shannon fled to her room before Oliver changed his mind and decided he needed her to watch Ollie.

As she stood in the bedroom with the pale yellow walls and lace curtains, Shannon felt a twinge of unease. She hadn't realized how personal bringing her stuff into a man's home would feel. Though she and Oliver wouldn't be sleeping in the same room, she was supremely aware that his bed was just on the other side of the wall.

Shopping at the Superette had also felt intimate. Almost as if they were a couple, instead of just employer and employee. Part of it, she knew, was because instead of simply going in and grabbing a few things, they'd strolled up and down the aisle chatting with various friends and family.

She'd seen the look of surprise on the faces of the people they'd run across. Oliver must have seen it, too, because he made a point of explaining she was Ollie's nanny. Still, some had continued to look skeptical.

After all, Oliver was hardly treating her like an employee, laughing and joking and giving her almost carte blanche on choosing what they needed.

Then he'd surprised her by insisting on bagging the groceries. When they reached home, he carried the items inside. Had she even thanked him? She paused, a pair of lace panties in her hand, and tried to recall.

Though her door was partially open, a knock sounded.

"Come in," she said absently and turned.

Oliver stood in the doorway, an odd expression on his face.

It took her a second to realize he wasn't looking at her. His gaze was riveted to the black thong dangling from her fingers.

Lightning fast, Shannon whirled and dropped the scrap of lingerie into the drawer. She cleared her throat. "I was just unpacking."

"I saw."

She flushed.

"Ollie is in his cot." Oliver's gaze slid to the open dresser drawer. "I thought I'd take a quick shower but wanted to make sure you didn't need the facilities first."

Shannon shoved aside the thought of him wet and naked and her wet and naked with him. She shut the drawer. "I'm fine. I'll just be unpacking."

He gave a curt nod and turned to leave, but stopped when she said his name.

"Uh, hey, I just wanted to say thanks for everything." She waved a vague hand in the air, but his confused look told Shannon she needed to be more specific. "For putting fresh sheets on my bed. For having the house so clean and organized. For your assistance at the Superette. I didn't expect you to pack up the groceries or carry them inside."

His brows pulled together in puzzlement. "I've learned that taking care of Oliver and the home is a daunting task.

Be assured I shall attempt to lessen the burden on you as much as possible."

Shannon stared at him for a long moment. Who was this man? She thought she'd had a good handle on Oliver Fortune Hayes, but she was beginning to think she didn't know him at all.

Almost of their own accord, her feet crossed the room to where he stood. Without giving herself a chance to think, she placed her hands on his forearms and brushed a kiss across his mouth. "Thank you."

He visibly stiffened. "What's going on, Shannon?"

She took a casual step back. "I'm not sure what you mean."

"The kiss." A muscle in Oliver's jaw jumped. "You made a point of insisting we keep things between us strictly business. I agreed. I gave you my word."

Embarrassment heated her cheeks. She wasn't an impulsive person and had no idea what had gotten into her. "Technically that wasn't a kiss."

Obviously confused, Oliver cocked his head.

"Take your shower." She patted his cheek. "And trust me. If I ever do kiss you, *really* kiss you, you'll know it."

Over the next few days, Oliver and Shannon settled into a routine. There was no touching or kissing, but neither was ever far from his mind. He made a concerted effort not to dwell on such matters because he didn't want to screw up what was turning out to be an extremely satisfying business arrangement.

In the span of a few short days, Shannon had turned a small, slightly battered house into a home. The smell of baking bread often greeted him when he awoke. Ollie was always fed, bathed and entertained. Oliver didn't take any of this for granted.

The initial plan was for her to be off duty at five, but Shannon insisted he sleep until he woke. When he got up, supper would be waiting. She insisted she loved to cook and had discovered it was fun to make dinner for someone besides herself.

But this evening they wouldn't be eating at home. They'd been invited to her parents' house for dinner. When Lilian had called, Oliver had attempted to decline the invitation, but had felt sorry for her when she told him Shep had sprained his ankle and was making her life miserable. She needed company, a distraction for Shep.

Oliver suggested Shannon go alone but Lilian said quite seriously that her husband would behave better with another man in the house. Though he doubted Shep would be happy to see him, Oliver had reluctantly accepted the invitation.

Now he was faced with what to wear. He glanced into his closet. If he wore a suit he'd be overdressed. He pulled out a pair of dark trousers and a charcoal shirt. But when he saw his reflection in the mirror, Oliver realized he needed to go even more casual.

With one last longing look at his suits, he changed into a pair of jeans and a thin-striped cotton shirt. He pulled out a pair of leather dress boots. Ignoring his unease, Oliver reminded himself this was suitable attire for dinner at a Horseback Hollow ranch.

When he came out of his bedroom shortly before they had to leave, Oliver was surprised to see Shannon wearing a maroon dress with heeled boots.

"You look lovely…and I'm underdressed."

She grabbed his arm when he spun to head back to his room to change.

"You're perfect," she said with obvious sincerity. "You'll

put my dad at ease. You know he'll be wearing jeans and one of his flannel shirts."

Oliver narrowed his gaze. "If dinner is casual, why are you wearing a dress?"

Her cheeks pinked. "Mom got on me the other day about my appearance. She said every time she saw me lately, I looked more like a ranch hand than a young woman."

Oliver's gaze slowly slid down her figure, the curves nicely emphasized by the clingy fabric of the dress.

"You could never look like a boy," he said honestly.

She looked totally feminine and all too appealing. She wore a new scent, a sultry fragrance that reminded him of tangled limbs and sweat-soaked sheets.

"I like your new perfume," he said as he helped her on with her jacket.

The pink on her cheeks deepened. "Rachel helped me pick it out. There's going to be some new guys at the progressive dinner on Saturday. She says I'm never going to attract anyone smelling like vanilla."

"Progressive dinner?"

"It's where you have cocktails at one house, appetizers at another, salads at yet another, et cetera," she explained. "Jensen and Amber are organizing it all. I believe they're doing the entrée at their place."

Oliver lifted Ollie from the floor, ignoring his howl of protest. "Who are these new men?"

"Friends of Quinn," Shannon said absently, scooping up Ollie's tiger and handing it to his son. "That's all I know."

"I look forward to meeting them," Oliver said smoothly.

Shannon blinked. "I didn't realize you were going."

Oliver smiled. "Wouldn't miss it for the world."

Chapter Nine

"You actually took Oliver home for dinner?" Rachel gave a hoot of laughter, the sound so light and carefree that Shannon couldn't help but smile.

From his perch in the high chair next to their table at the Vicker's Corners ice cream shop, Ollie looked up from rearranging his Cheerios cereal. He garbled out a smattering of words.

Since the boy had eaten all but ten of the "Os," Shannon grabbed the Tupperware container from her purse and put a few more on the table.

"It wasn't so bad," Shannon said, recalling the evening that had started off a bit awkwardly but ended quite well. "Oliver loves my mom's cooking, and he and my dad talked horses. Apparently Oliver not only has a stable of Arabians at his country estate, he also owns a couple of racehorses."

"From what I've heard he's got big bucks. I'm sure he

owns a lot more than a few horses." Rachel leaned forward, resting her forearms on the table. "Has he kissed you yet?"

"No," Shannon answered quite honestly. "He's been a perfect gentleman."

She saw no need to add that *she'd* kissed *him*. Despite the havoc it had wreaked on her sleep, that brief one-time brush against his lips barely counted.

"Is he gay?"

"No, he's not gay, he's British." Shannon saw Rachel's lips twitch. She met her friend's gaze. "Sometimes when we're together, I can almost feel the heat between us scorch my skin, but he always shuts it down."

Rachel took a long, thoughtful sip of her soda. "Why do you think that is?"

"My fault. I insisted we keep things strictly business." For a second Shannon dropped her gaze to her hands, before focusing back on Rachel. "I still believe it's for the best."

"Seriously?" Rachel's disbelieving expression was almost comical.

"Yes, seriously. Think how awkward it would be if we hopped into bed together," Shannon pointed out.

"Honey, I'm betting the guy is fairly experienced in the bedroom. I don't think there would be much awkwardness."

"You thought he was gay."

Rachel dismissed this with a flick of her wrist. "I was just trying to get a reaction."

"Like you're doing now."

"Guilty as charged." Rachel sounded not at all sorry as she slurped up the last of her Italian soda.

"If we *did* have a physical relationship, then decide it's a mistake, I'd have to face him every day."

"You're a big girl. You could handle it."

"I don't know, Rachel. He's different from other guys I've dated. There's something about him that—"

"Mama." Ollie reached over and tugged on Shannon's sleeve, then repeated more loudly. "Mama."

Rachel gave an incredulous laugh. "Did the munchkin just call you 'Mama'?"

"It's his word for any woman." She turned to Ollie. "What is it you want, sweet pea?"

"Dink." He pointed to her malt. "Dink."

"You want a drink, sweet boy? What do you say?"

"Pease." Ollie batted his lashes. He had his father's charm in spades, Shannon decided, and let him sip from her straw.

"That kid has you wrapped around his little finger," Rachel said with a sly smile.

"I'm falling hard for both of them, Rachel," Shannon admitted with a heavy sigh. "And I can't seem to do a thing to stop it."

The one thing she'd done right, Shannon decided that Saturday evening, was not attend the progressive dinner with Oliver. When he asked if she wanted to go with him, she'd told him she planned to ride with Rachel.

She and Rachel had decided that in the ice cream shop several days earlier. Her friend insisted it would be good for Oliver to not take her for granted. From Shannon's perspective, it was all about making the two of them seem less like a couple. Not only in the mind of the community, but in hers, as well.

Oliver would soon be returning to England. Once he left, she'd likely never see him or Ollie again. She couldn't afford to get too attached.

"These Crazy Coyote Margaritas are de-lish," Rachel said, sipping hers.

"They're good...and strong." Shannon couldn't recall the last time she'd had a drink where the alcohol was so prominent. "We'd better pace ourselves."

"Let's pace ourselves right over to those two hunky cowboys Quinn invited."

"Doesn't that seem a bit bold to you?"

"The early bird gets the worm."

"Yeah, and the early worm gets eaten."

Rachel merely shot her a saucy smile. When she started across the room, Shannon hurried to catch up. Rachel looked adorable in her black skinny jeans and a color-block sweater. Shannon had chosen a wrap dress of emerald green but wondered if she should have worn pants tonight instead.

The two men speaking with Quinn were strangers. Shannon had heard through the singles grapevine that both were unattached and each owned large ranches in central Texas.

She and Rachel had almost reached the men, when she felt a hand on her arm. She paused but Rachel continued on without her, obviously wanting dibs on the cowboy of her choice.

"Fancy meeting you here."

Shannon turned and immediately found herself drowning in the liquid depths of Oliver's blue eyes.

"Hello, Oliver."

He looked terrific in dark trousers and a gray shirt. He smelled terrific. Not a scent she recognized but it was nice, very nice. And the spot where his hand now rested on her arm sent waves of heat throughout her body.

"You look lovely." His gaze traveled all the way down from her face to the tips of her heeled boots. "You should wear that color more often."

"I'll keep that in mind." Get off the personal, she told

herself. "How did Ollie do when you dropped him off at your mother's?"

Josephine had been thrilled when Oliver had asked her to watch Ollie overnight. It would be the first time the toddler had spent the night since arriving in Horseback Hollow. Though Oliver hadn't appeared concerned, Shannon was worried.

A troubled look appeared in his eyes. "He cried. I felt like a heel walking out the door and leaving him there."

"I wonder how he's doing."

"Better. I called before I came in. Mum said they were playing with his trucks." Oliver expelled a breath. "Bedtime may be difficult."

Shannon had gotten into the habit of rocking Ollie to sleep at night. She knew she should probably just put him in his crib—or cot as Oliver liked to call it—and let him cry. But he'd been through so much in his young life, and the closeness seemed to comfort him. "Did you tell your mother he likes to be rocked to sleep?"

"I did." His lips tightened. "I got the feeling she thought it unnecessary."

When someone took her empty glass and handed her another Crazy Coyote, Shannon accepted it automatically. "I hope she at least gives it a try."

"I hope so, as well."

"What are you two talking about?" Jude stopped beside them, one arm looped around Gabi's shoulders. "You look way too serious."

"Nothing important," Oliver said smoothly.

"Those Crazy Coyotes pack a punch," Gabi said to Shannon. "Watch yourself."

Shannon glanced down, surprised to find the second drink in her hand. "I will. But I'm safe anyway. Rachel is the designated driver."

"Rachel?" Gabi glanced curiously at Oliver. "You two didn't come together?"

"Nope," Shannon said, taking a gulp of her drink.

Gabi frowned. "How odd."

"Not so odd, sweetheart." Jude smiled. "Shannon works for Oliver. They're not dating."

Though she couldn't have said it better herself, for some reason the words stung.

The fact that Oliver merely sipped his glass of wine, his eyes dark and unreadable, only made it worse.

Time to seek out Rachel and those two gorgeous cowboys. Men who'd grown up in Texas and would *stay* in Texas. One of them was bound to be just the kind of man she was looking for.

But as Shannon crossed the room, she found her mind drifting to the two men she couldn't have, one a handsome charmer with dark hair and wicked blue eyes, the other a miniversion of the first, a little boy with a toothy grin who called her "Mama."

Oliver watched Shannon flirt and laugh with a tall blond-haired cowboy at every house on the progressive dinner circuit. The evening was coming to a close, and by the way the guy was looking at Shannon, baked Alaska wasn't the only thing he wanted for dessert this evening.

He'd started the evening with a glass of wine but had since switched to water. Not Shannon.

In addition to dessert, Christopher and his fiancée, Kinsley, had made a variety of after-dinner drinks available to their guests.

Not only had Shannon drank a couple of Crazy Coyote Margaritas earlier, she'd enjoyed wine with dinner and had another glass in her hand now. The cowboy, Oliver noted, had switched to coffee.

Though Oliver told himself Shannon wasn't his concern, there was something about the man he didn't like. When they'd been introduced, he'd noticed an arrogant immaturity, a meanness that he hid quite well behind a charming smile.

"Your nanny and the cowboy look like they're having a good time," Jensen observed, coming to stand beside him and noting the direction of his gaze.

"Her name is Shannon." Even as he spoke with his brother, his gaze remained focused on her. He saw her glance around as if searching for someone. "She's looking for Rachel."

"Rachel left. I heard her tell Kinsley she wasn't feeling well."

"She was Shannon's ride home."

"Rachel probably assumed you'd take her home." Jensen took a sip of wine, gazed up at his brother. "Or the cowboy."

Oliver's lips tightened. "I don't like the way he's looking at her."

"You mean like she's a piece of meat and he hasn't eaten in a week?"

"Excellent summation."

"What are you going to do about it?"

Oliver exhaled a ragged breath and turned away. "Nothing. Shannon's personal life is her business. Not mine."

That feeling lasted until it was time to leave and he headed toward his car. Most of the others had already left, but he'd stayed behind to speak with Chris about the work of the Fortune Foundation.

There was a shiny red pickup truck parked not far from his car. As Oliver drew closer to his car, voices resounded in the still night air.

He realized one of those voices was Shannon's. Oliver stopped and listened, his fingers on his key fob.

"I told you no."

There was frustration in her voice. Anger, too. And fear?

"C'mon, you've been teasin' me all night. No need to play the shy virgin."

"I don't want you to touch me. No. Wesley, stop."

Oliver saw red. Not even conscious of covering the last few feet to the truck, he jerked the door open and yanked the cowboy off Shannon.

Taken by surprise, the man fell to the ground with a hard thud.

"Are you okay?" he asked Shannon, her eyes too bright and her face pale.

She nodded, her lips trembling.

The cowboy was now on his feet, hands clenched into fists at his sides. "What the hel—"

Oliver took a step toward the man. He wasn't a street fighter but he had displayed a talent for boxing in his younger years. He resisted—but barely—the urge to tear the man apart. "When a lady says no, she means no."

The man's mouth turned sulky. "We were just havin' us a little fun."

"When a lady says no, she means no," Oliver repeated, his words like ice.

By now Shannon had scrambled from the car and moved so that she stood behind him.

"I don't have a beef with you." Wesley raked a hand through his shaggy blond hair. His gaze slid to Shannon. "Didn't mean no disrespect."

Oliver watched as Wesley turned, jumped back in his truck and roared off.

"There goes my ride."

Oliver whirled and gave an incredulous laugh. "You're upset he's not driving you home?"

"It was a joke." Shannon offered a shaky smile. "A poor one."

He extended his hand to her. "Let me take you home."

"He wouldn't listen to me." Her lips began to tremble in earnest now. Tears welled in her eyes. "I think if you hadn't come along, he might have…" She faltered, her breath coming in gasps. "He might have—"

Suddenly Oliver's arms wrapped around her and he pulled her to him, holding her tight while her tears drenched his shoulder. "He didn't. Shh. You're okay."

The words were soft and gentle, as soothing as the ones he said to Ollie when the boy cried. Thankfully, the man hadn't injured her. Or had he?

"Did he hurt you?" Oliver asked abruptly, holding her at arm's length, his gaze desperately searching her still-moist eyes.

"My wrist." She held up her right hand and he could see the red marks from pressure. "But no, I'm okay."

She trembled all over now; even her teeth chattered. "Could you hold me again? J-just for a s-second. I'm s-s-so c-cold."

"Certainly."

With great gentleness, Oliver wrapped his arms around her and held her close. Her body fit perfectly against his.

They stood there in the quiet, with the full moon shining overhead and the crickets chirping, until the trembling and the tears subsided.

She was the one who broke the connection, sniffling and swiping at her eyes as she took a step back. "I—I'm sorry."

"He's the one who should be sorry," Oliver said, a grim

note in his voice. "And he will be. I doubt Quinn will want to do business with him once he hears about this incident."

"Oh, Oliver, please don't tell Quinn." She lifted her pleading gaze to his. "I shouldn't have kissed him. It—it gave him ideas and—"

"You listen to me, Shannon Singleton, and listen carefully. There is no excuse for a man to force himself on a woman. You said no. You said stop. I heard you and he heard you, too. He chose not to listen."

"He wouldn't listen," she said morosely. "No one ever listens."

"Not people like him." Oliver pressed his lips together and fought for control over his anger. "I know his type. All charm and full of compliments, underneath cold calculation. He saw you, he wanted you, and by God he was going to have you…regardless of your feelings on the matter."

Shannon pressed a hand to her belly. "I feel sick."

Without warning, she sprinted to the bushes and was violently ill.

When she returned, looking pale as death, he handed her a precisely folded handkerchief.

A ghost of a smile lifted her lips. "Where'd this come from?"

"My pocket," he told her. "A gentleman never leaves home without a handkerchief."

His words had the desired effect of bringing a smile to her lips.

"I believe—" Oliver held out his arm to her "—it's time to head home."

She met his gaze. "There's nowhere else I'd rather be."

Chapter Ten

Shannon kept her eyes closed during the trip home. She couldn't believe what a mess she'd made of the evening. For a second, before Oliver had pulled Wes off her, she feared she wouldn't be able to stop him.

There had been something in the cowboy's gaze only seconds before Oliver had arrived that had chilled her to the bone. For a second white-hot terror resurfaced and threatened to overwhelm. Nothing happened, she reminded herself. Still, she shivered.

"You're shaking." Beneath the calm, well-modulated tone, Shannon heard the concern. "Shall I turn on the heater?"

"The temperature is fine." Even as she said the words, her teeth began to chatter.

Oliver shook his head. He pulled the car to the side of the country road. Reaching over into the backseat, he grabbed a jacket. "Put this on."

She didn't argue. Shannon shrugged into the cashmere coat and let the comforting warmth surround her. The exquisite softness coupled with the faint scent of Oliver's cologne that clung to the jacket soothed her jangled nerves. By the time they'd gone a couple of miles, the trembling stilled.

Oliver had been amazing; a white knight riding—well, more like running—to her rescue. He'd stood strong against Wesley, stared the cowboy straight in the eye and told him what he did—what he'd been about to do—was wrong.

Now, being with Oliver in the luxurious confines of the car with the strains of classical music playing on the radio, Shannon felt as if nothing could ever harm her. Not as long as Oliver was with her.

When they pulled into the driveway, relief washed over her. She was home.

Shannon wasn't sure exactly when she'd started thinking of the old ranch house as home, but it didn't matter. This was another place she felt safe.

"Thank you, Oliver." She unbuckled her belt and shifted to face him. "For everything."

He surprised her by leaning close and cupping her face in his broad palm. "I'll never let anything—or anyone—hurt you."

The fierceness of his tone was at odds with his gentle touch.

Her heart thudded against her chest so loudly it was a wonder he couldn't hear.

Or perhaps he did. Oliver's hand dropped away and he sat back. "Let's go inside. You've had a long day."

When he opened her car door, Shannon stepped out, slipping her hands into the pockets of the jacket.

His palm rested lightly against the small of her back

as they traversed the short distance to the house. Barnaby met them at the door, wagging his tail and offering several welcoming woofs before racing outside.

While the corgi's welcome had been loud and exuberant, without Ollie, the house seemed too quiet.

Seconds later, Oliver let Barnaby back inside. The corgi did his best to herd Shannon deeper into the house, but her feet remained firmly rooted in the foyer. She knew she was stalling, but couldn't bear the thought of going to her bedroom and being alone with her thoughts.

"How are Ollie and your mother getting along?" she asked, conscious of Oliver's concerned gaze riveted on her.

"Step into the kitchen and have a seat. I'll tell you everything I know." Oliver gestured to the table. "It's a fascinating tale."

The kind understanding in his eyes told her he knew exactly why she was hesitating. Her heart swelled in gratitude.

"I want to hear it all. He's been on my mind all evening." Right now, it felt good to focus on someone other than herself.

Oliver crossed the room, flipped on the lights in the kitchen and then turned back to Shannon. "May I get you a cup of tea? I have chamomile infusion. It has no caffeine. According to Amelia, drinking it before bedtime practically guarantees happy dreams."

Though Shannon's stomach was still unsettled, he looked so eager to comfort her, she couldn't refuse. "I'd love some."

As Oliver proceeded to fill the kettle, Shannon finally got her feet to move. She glanced longingly at the sofa, but her mouth held a foul taste.

"I'm going to freshen up a bit," she told Oliver.

"Take your time. The tea will need to steep."

She felt his gaze follow her as she headed to the bathroom. After brushing her teeth, she splashed her face with cold water and got rid of the raccoon smudges below her eyes. Obviously waterproof mascara wasn't the same as tear-proof.

Shannon pinched her cheeks to add color to the pallor, then sat on the edge of the tub and took off her boots and tights. Her legs were bare when she padded back into the living room. She hung up his cashmere storm jacket then took a seat at the table.

Oliver kept the conversation light until he handed her a steaming mug emblazoned with Don't Mess With Texas.

Wrapping her hands around the ceramic, she gave him a grateful smile while he sat across from her.

"You look as if you're feeling better."

"I am." Even as she said the words, Shannon realized they were true. She rested her elbows on the table and fixed her gaze on Oliver. "Now, tell me all about Ollie's evening."

"According to Mum, it was a bit of a rocky road at first. He kept crying out for 'Mama.'" Oliver's brows pulled together. "It's difficult for me to believe he meant Diane. From everything I heard, she hadn't spent much time with him those last few months. And she's been gone for some time now."

"He calls me 'Mama' sometimes," Shannon admitted. "I think it's a term he uses for women in general."

"I wasn't aware…" Oliver rubbed his chin. "That explains a lot."

"Did he finally settle down? Have fun?"

"Ah, yes, indeed he did." Oliver seemed to shake off whatever thoughts had pulled him away and refocused on her.

"Tell me," she prompted. "I want deets."

"Deets?" He lifted a brow.

She laughed. "Details."

"Ollie ate well," Oliver told her, sipping his tea. "Mum said he appeared to enjoy all the attention. He asked for Barnaby numerous times."

Hearing the sound of his name, the corgi rose from his dog bed, stretched and then moved to Shannon.

"Good boy." She patted his head and gave him a brief scratch behind his ears.

Oliver watched the interaction with interest, smiling when the dog finally left Shannon to mosey over to him.

"I checked with my mother right before I left the party. She said Ollie went to sleep—after being rocked, I might add—and was sleeping like an angel." Oliver's gaze took on a faraway look. "She told me many times how much she enjoyed having him over."

"Sounds like you may have a babysitter for life."

He lifted the mug of tea, appearing to consider the statement. "While I'm in Horseback Hollow, anyway."

Shannon's heart plummeted. It was so easy to forget that Oliver didn't belong here, to think this was his home. To imagine him being here forever. With her.

But he wouldn't be staying and putting down roots. In fact, by the first of April he'd be back in London. She'd likely never see him again.

It was something she had to keep in mind, or an April Fool's Day joke would be on her.

First thing the next morning Oliver called Quinn. He'd promised the sleeping beauty in the other room that he wouldn't tell Quinn what had gone on last night. And he kept his promise. But that didn't mean he couldn't let Quinn know that his potential business partner was a scoundrel of the first order.

While Oliver scrambled eggs and fried bacon, he issued his warning in words that had been carefully chosen prior to placing the call.

As expected, Quinn pressed for solid details. Oliver only reiterated if he was going into business with someone, Wesley should never be considered, no matter how perfect a partner he appeared to be on paper.

Oliver heard Amelia in the background telling Quinn that her brother rarely issued such warnings and they should heed it. He appreciated his sister's confidence and support. By the time he ended the call, Oliver felt certain he'd squashed any business deal between Quinn and Wesley.

"Good morning."

Oliver slid the phone into his pocket and glanced up. Shannon stood in the hallway, looking a bit heavy-eyed— but just as beautiful as always—in jeans, a long-sleeved T-shirt and cowboy boots. Her hair, normally loose around her shoulders, had been woven into some sort of complicated braid.

He rose from the table. "Would you like some breakfast?"

"I believe that's supposed to be my line." A smile lifted the corners of her lips. "But I have a different question for you this morning."

Intrigued, Oliver inclined his head. "What is it?"

"You like horses, right?"

"I do. Very much."

"I just spoke with my mother." Shannon shifted uncertainly from one foot to the other. "My dad's ankle isn't any better. It seems to be a pretty bad sprain."

"I'm sorry to hear it." Oliver was not only sorry for Shep but for Lilian, as well. It couldn't be easy keeping an active man like Shep Singleton down.

"The thing is, my parents ride every day. It's something they've done for years." Shannon crossed the room and picked a piece of crisp bacon from the frying pan. "Knowing Ollie would be at your mother's this morning, she asked if I would come over and exercise the horses. If we went together, both horses would get a workout. It wouldn't take long."

There had been a period, years ago, when Oliver had ridden every day. Once he moved to London, riding had been confined to visits to his country estate. He'd missed it, he realized.

"My mother said she'd like to keep Ollie all morning," Oliver mused.

"We'd easily be there to pick him up by noon."

Oliver thought, considered. There were things he needed to do to prepare for his workday. But he sensed Shannon needed a ride in the great outdoors more than she needed almost anything else.

He glanced down at his dark trousers and dress shirt. "Give me five minutes to change and I'll be ready."

Shannon reined the horse to a halt at the top of a hill that overlooked a large swath of her parents' property. Though the sun shone brightly, the temperature was in the upper sixties, perfect riding weather.

Beside her, Oliver sat easily on her father's horse, a spirited roan named Bucky. Right before he mounted Bucky, she'd plopped a black cowboy hat on his head.

He'd muttered a protest, but she knew it was only for form when he'd left on the Stetson headgear. Though comfortable outside, the sun could be intense to an unshielded head.

They'd ambled through fields, then galloped together down a well-worn path by the stream. When they'd reached the hill—okay, so it was more of a small mound—she enticed him to the top by telling him the view would be worth it.

"What do you think?" She relaxed in the saddle, gazing out over the valley where cattle grazed.

"Beautiful."

"That's what I think—" But when Shannon turned, thrilled he saw the peaceful serenity and beauty that many overlooked, she realized his gaze wasn't on the land, but on her.

Her face had to be dusty, her hat tipped back, and some of the hair that she'd woven into a side braid now hung loose against her cheek. Not to mention her eyes had to be puffy from last night. But the way he looked at her, well, she couldn't remember any man looking at her in quite the same way.

Her heart swelled until she thought it would burst from her chest. "Thank you."

A startled look crossed his face. "For what?"

"For being so nice to me."

"I don't understand."

"You were my knight in shining armor last night." Shannon refused to let embarrassment quash the words she desperately needed to say. "You saved me from an evil sorcerer. You comforted me. Not once did you make me feel stupid, though I had been very stupid."

"No," he said forcefully. "What happened was all on him."

"I just want you to know that I appreciated you coming to my rescue and being so…nice. If there's anything I can ever do for you, all you need to do is say the word and I'm there."

"Thanks is hardly necessary," he began. "I—"

"It's very necessary," she insisted. "I also realize what

you gave up to come here today. Being on horseback under the bright blue skies has made me feel better. You knew it would."

"How could anyone not feel better with all this beauty as far as the eye can see?" He gestured with one hand, though his gaze remained on her.

"You're a special guy, Oliver. I hope one day you find a woman back in London who can appreciate all you have to offer."

"This is the one," Rachel said with the authority of a seasoned shopper. "It's you."

Shannon studied the simple, yet sexy, black dress. All evening they'd searched for just the right dress for Shannon to wear to the Grand Fortune wedding ceremony Friday night.

When one Fortune got married it was a big deal. But when four Fortune siblings decided to tie the knot on the same day, the event took on epic status. The evening would be the talk of the year, no, the decade. Not just any dress would do for such a wedding.

The stores in Lubbock had an abundance of dresses in every style and color. A few had caught Shannon's eye enough to try them on. But none had jumped out and proclaimed, "I am the one."

They'd headed back to Horseback Hollow, empty-handed and discouraged. At the last minute they decided to check out a couple of boutiques in Vicker's Corners.

At boutique number two, they hit the jackpot. Amazed, Shannon gazed at her reflection in the triple mirror. "It makes me look positively skinny."

"Forget skinny. It makes your boobs look ginormous," Rachel said, and the sales clerk laughed.

"The dress is very flattering," the clerk concurred. "Is this for a special Valentine's date?"

"Actually," Shannon said, "I'm attending a wedding on Valentine's Day."

"Ah, *the* wedding. Wear that dress and your date won't be able to take his eyes off you," the clerk assured her before hurrying off to help another customer.

"She's right." Rachel relaxed in the dressing room chair while Shannon slipped off the dress. "It's perfect for the weddings."

Rachel's overemphasis of the plural made Shannon smile.

"Seriously," Rachel continued, "how often do you get one dress that will cover four weddings?"

Shannon slanted a glance at the price tag and tried not to wince. While the cost was definitely more than she wanted to spend, the dress *was* gorgeous. She thought about the clerk's words.

Would Oliver think she was lovely? Would he look at her—

"Especially four Fortune weddings."

Shannon reined in her thoughts. While she'd been daydreaming, Rachel had been chattering about the upcoming nuptials.

"I don't know about you," Rachel continued, "but I wouldn't want to share my special day with three other couples."

"It wouldn't be for me," Shannon acknowledged. "But I think the Fortune siblings must view this grand event as even more special because they're sharing it with the ones they love."

"I bet Jeanne Marie and Deke are celebrating."

Shannon raised a brow.

"Think about it, four weddings for the price of one," Rachel explained. "What a deal."

"For them maybe," Shannon said with a laugh. "I'm just grateful you agreed to go in with me on four gifts."

On Friday, at Jeanne Marie and Deke's sprawling ranch, four of their children would say their vows: Jude and Gabi and Chris and Kinsley, as well as Stacey Fortune Jones marrying Colton Foster and Liam Fortune Jones marrying Julia Tierney.

They'd had the large red barn on their property converted into a reception area. Outside, a huge stage had been constructed for the ceremony itself. Shannon had no doubt the quadruple wedding ceremony and reception would be a night to remember in Horseback Hollow.

"Did I tell you my parents are watching Ollie?" Shannon stepped out of the dress and handed it to Rachel.

"Your parents are such good friends of Deke and Jeanne Marie." Rachel placed the dress on the padded hanger, a look of surprise in her eyes. "I thought for sure they'd be invited."

"They are close friends and they planned to go." Shannon pulled on her jeans and tucked in her shirt. "But my dad's ankle is still bothering him. Because it's so difficult for him to get around, they decided to stay home."

Shannon reached down to pick up her bag. When she straightened, she found Rachel staring at her with a curious expression.

"What's wrong?" she asked her friend.

"I know we've planned to go together for ages." Rachel spoke slowly, as if choosing her words carefully. "But if you'd rather go with Oliver…"

"No. No way. I'll have more fun with you." The moment the words left her lips, Shannon wished she could pull them back. It sounded as if she was dissing Oliver, when nothing could be further from the truth.

She'd only meant to reassure Rachel their plans were solid and she wasn't doing a last-minute about-face.

"You're right. He may be hot but he's a little uptight." Rachel spoke cheerily, her good humor back. "Did you hear that all four of Gabi's brothers will be there? Orlando showed me pictures the other day. All I can say is, wow. Not a dog in the bunch. Tall. Dark. Hunky. They look like fun guys. We should consider hanging with them at the reception."

"Perhaps." Shannon did her best to summon some enthusiasm even though the only hunky man she wanted to hang with was Oliver.

Of course, Oliver would soon be an ocean away. She supposed it wouldn't hurt to consider other possibilities.

But even as the thought crossed her mind, Shannon knew she wasn't interested. There was only one man she wanted. Only one man she loved. And that man was the one who could never be hers.

Chapter Eleven

After making sure his tie was precisely knotted, Oliver strode down the hall. When he reached the living room, he came to an abrupt stop. For a second, all he could do was gaze at the vision of loveliness in black lace before him.

Shannon had bent over to give Ollie a toy. The angle gave Oliver an excellent view of her breasts—er, her dress. In his thirty-seven years, Oliver had seen his share of short black dresses. Cocktail parties, gallery openings and charity galas were filled with women wearing what many considered the classic party dress. Never had he seen one that took his breath away.

Though it didn't show an obscene amount of skin, something in the cut of the dress made Shannon's legs look longer, her waist impossibly tiny and her breasts…

His mouth went dry. When he cleared his throat, hoping to get some fluid to the area, she straightened and shot him a brilliant smile.

Then her beautiful eyes widened.

"Oh, my." She pretended to fan herself. "You're really rockin' that black suit, mister."

For the weddings of his four cousins, Oliver had chosen a slim-fit Armani, coupling it with a crisp white shirt and dark skinny tie. His favorite pair of Paul Smith black oxfords completed the outfit.

Though the phrase "rockin' that suit" wasn't familiar, the admiration in her eyes said she approved of his choice of attire.

"Your dress," he said, unable to keep his gaze from dropping to the lacy vee that showed the ivory swell of her breasts, "is…unbelievable."

"In a good way, I hope?" Though her tone was light, he saw concern in the brown depths of her eyes.

"You will be the prettiest woman there."

She gave a pleased laugh and lifted Ollie into her arms. "That's nice to hear, but with four gorgeous brides, I sincerely doubt that."

"The prettiest woman there," he repeated, happy her plans to attend with her friend had fallen through and she was his for the night.

A flush rose up her neck, but he saw his words had pleased her. She dropped her gaze to Ollie, who was attempting to pull the tiny silver necklace from her neck.

"Did you hear that, Ollie?" she asked the toddler. "Your daddy thinks I'm pretty."

With chubby fingers still wrapped around the necklace, Ollie lifted his gaze and stared at her for several seconds. He grinned.

"Pretty Mama," he said clearly, then repeated the words. "Pretty Mama."

Oliver stared, startled.

"I think you have another admirer," was the best he could manage.

"Yeah," she said with a self-deprecating smile. "I'm a big hit with the toddler set."

"He called you 'Mama.'"

"That's his go-to word for females," she reminded him.

Oliver didn't argue but he was fairly certain Ollie knew exactly who he was calling "Mama." He glanced at his watch. "We should leave."

"You're right. It's not going to be quick and easy getting away from my parents." Shannon offered a wry smile. "Be prepared. They'll want you to go through Ollie's bedtime routine in excruciating detail."

She never overstepped, Oliver thought. Shannon always made it clear Ollie was ultimately his son, his responsibility, not hers. The trouble was, Shannon was such a natural with him it was easy for him to forget.

Mrs. Crowder, his London nanny, was efficient and kind to his son. But Ollie had never called her "Mama." He wondered if the older woman rocked Ollie to sleep every night or sang silly songs with him. These were things Shannon did as part of the daily routine. Oliver made a mental note to pay more attention to those details once he was back in London.

On the drive to her parents' ranch, Ollie and Shannon sang a song about monkeys jumping on the bed. Actually Shannon did most of the singing, with Ollie occasionally yelling out "no more" or "monkey" several beats too late.

The foolishness of the tune coupled with the sound of his son's giggles made Oliver smile.

As Shannon had predicted, Shep and Lilian wouldn't let them leave until they'd been apprised of every nuance of Ollie's schedule. When they returned to the car, Oliver had no doubt his son would be well cared for during the evening.

"That was kind of your parents to offer to keep Ollie overnight." Oliver exited the long drive and turned the car in the direction of Jeanne Marie and Deke's ranch.

"My parents adore children." A tiny smile lifted her lips. "They can't wait to have grandchildren. Watching Ollie gives them a taste of what that will someday be like."

"Happy to be of service."

Shannon's expression turned thoughtful. "I'm glad you brought Ollie to Horseback Hollow. It's good he had this chance to get acquainted with your family and them with him."

Oliver realized with a sense of chagrin that he'd never thought of the trip in those terms. In his mind, coming to Texas had been about seeing Amelia and meeting his new niece.

"Thanks to modern technology, even after you return to London you'll be able to video chat with your mother and other family members," Shannon continued. "That way they can stay close to Ollie."

"Good suggestion." But Oliver found he didn't want to talk about leaving Horseback Hollow. Not tonight. "Do you like weddings?"

Shannon blinked at the abrupt change of subject but went with the flow.

"What woman doesn't? I enjoy seeing the dresses and the hair. I like seeing what kind of flowers the bride and groom chose and how they structured the ceremony." She paused for a second. "With four brides and grooms, I wonder how they decided everything. Majority vote?"

Oliver lifted a shoulder in a slight shrug.

"I can see the advantages of all of them getting married at the same time but…" This time, it was her turn to shrug.

"Not for you?"

"Never say never," she said with a little laugh, "but I don't believe it would be for me. Anyway, marriage is so far down the road for me it doesn't even bear thinking about."

Oliver slanted a sideways glance. "You'll find the right man."

Having Oliver mention her with another man in the same breath gave Shannon a bad taste in her mouth. "When you married Diane, you must have thought she was the right one for you."

Oliver's only reaction was a tightening grip on the steering wheel. "At the time, I was convinced we made an excellent match. We socialized with the same people, had similar interests and backgrounds. I thought she'd be happy if I gave her what she wanted. I was mistaken."

His lips clamped shut.

"What did she want?" Shannon asked quietly into the stillness.

"What most women want—a lovely home, designer clothes, jewels."

"I'd settle for a man who loves me," Shannon murmured.

Oliver continued as if she hadn't spoken. Perhaps he hadn't heard her. His gaze had taken on a faraway look. "She wanted a child, so we had Ollie. He was an infant when she began a relationship with another man."

"She cheated on you?" Shannon's voice rose, despite her efforts to control it.

"She left me for him." Oliver spoke in a tone one might use to report an expected change in stock prices. "They were together approximately six months when she replaced him with the man she was with at the time she died."

"It sounds as if she wasn't sure what she wanted."

"Perhaps." His expression gave nothing away. "All I know for certain was she no longer wanted me. I couldn't make her happy."

"I'm sorry." Impulsively Shannon reached over and squeezed his hand.

"It was the failure of our marriage that bothered me more than losing her," he said almost to himself. "Up until our divorce, I believed if I worked hard enough at something, I would be successful."

Shannon heard the disappointment in his voice. She knew what it was like to not live up to your own expectations. If only she could pull him close and comfort him as he'd comforted her not all that long ago.

"I never heard what happened to your plans to attend the weddings with Rachel." By the change in subject, Oliver made it clear the discussion of his failed marriage had come to a close.

Shannon understood that, too. She often did the same thing when the subject of Jerry and how she'd handled that whole situation came up.

"Rach is supergood with hair. A couple of the brides asked if she'd come early to help with final touch-ups." Shannon waved a dismissive hand. "She was concerned about leaving me in the lurch, but I assured her it was no problem. I told her I'd probably catch a ride with you. If not, there was always Wesley."

His gaze shot to her. "Surely you would not consider—"

"Not in a bazillion years." She made a face. "I just wanted to see if you were listening."

"I always listen to you."

He'd listened to her that night when that scumbag had attacked her. And Oliver had held her while she cried...

"I've decided if Wesley is there tonight—" Shannon swallowed her trepidation and forced a bright smile "—I'll simply ignore him. There'll be so many people that it shouldn't be difficult."

"He won't be there."

The words were said with such confidence Shannon had no doubt they were true.

"How do you—" Shannon frowned. "You promised you wouldn't say anything about what happened to anyone."

"You should know by now I'm a man of my word," Oliver said stiffly, appearing affronted. "I didn't mention your name or any specific incident. I merely told Quinn that Wesley was not the type of man he should have as a business partner or a friend."

Incredulous, Shannon could only stare. "He didn't ask why you felt that way?"

"Of course he did." A slight smile lifted Oliver's lips. "But he quit pressing for details when Amelia told him to trust me."

"Oh."

"I would never betray your confidence. Or my promise to you." Oliver slanted a speculative glance in her direction. "Enough talk about that. Did I mention my brother Brodie will be attending the wedding?"

"I don't believe I've met him."

"He's flying in for the ceremony." A look of fondness crept into Oliver's gaze. "Knowing Brodie, he'll return to London as soon as possible."

As if sensing her curiosity, Oliver smiled. "Brodie enjoys the finer things in life. This town would not be his cup of tea. Too small and too rustic."

Shannon pulled her brows together, trying to remember the family history. "Is he older or younger than you?"

"Four years younger."

"That means he's between you and Jensen?"

"Yes. Brodie and I are from our mother's first marriage. Jensen is from her second."

Shannon tapped a finger against her lips. "I knew Jensen's father had died and Josephine was a widow. Is your dad still alive?"

"No."

There was a wealth of emotion contained in the single clipped word.

As irritating as her father could be at times, Shannon knew she'd be devastated if anything happened to him. She reached over and placed a hand on Oliver's arm. "I'm so sorry."

"Don't be. He was a mean SOB who was not liked by most people, including his sons."

"Then I'm doubly sorry," Shannon said softly. "Growing up with such a father had to be—"

"I consider my mother's second husband, Sir Simon Chesterfield, my father. He was a good man. The best, actually." Oliver met her gaze. "You don't have to be related by blood to be a parent."

"I agree." For some reason Shannon thought of Ollie. She could easily love him as if he were her own. Heck, she was already halfway in love with the little guy.

As the car slowed, Shannon glanced out the window. "Oh my goodness, look at all the people."

A man Shannon recognized as working for the Horseback Hollow Sheriff's Department motioned for Oliver to turn into a large field that was now a parking lot.

White golf carts, festively decorated with ribbons and fresh flowers, zipped up and down the rows of cars, transporting attendees to where the ceremony would be held. The drivers— many of them locals—looked quite impressive in black pants, crisp white shirts and red vests.

Shannon wasn't sure how many carts were running but

had a feeling anyone golfing today would be walking eighteen holes.

She waited for Oliver to help her out of the cart, anticipating the moment he'd take her hand and she'd get to touch him—however briefly—once again.

To her surprise—and pleasure—the contact wasn't short-lived. Instead of immediately releasing her fingers, he entwined his with hers and retained the hold while they waited for the cart. Unfortunately, once they stepped inside the open vehicle, he released her hand. But she felt encouraged when he rested his arm on the top of the seat.

"I hear Jeanne Marie and Deke had the interior of the barn completely renovated for the reception and dance," Shannon said as the large red structure came into view.

"Mum told me the work has been going on for weeks." As they drew close, Oliver's gaze lingered on the large number of people waiting to be seated. "Apparently the carpenters just finished the outdoor stage where the wedding ceremony will take place earlier this week."

"It's fortunate rain stayed out of the forecast."

"I have no doubt there was a contingency plan in case of bad weather."

"I can't wait to see what everyone in the wedding parties is wearing." Shannon could feel her excitement build the closer the cart got to the drop-off point. "I heard each bride has two attendants, a maid or matron of honor and a bridesmaid."

"More than adequate."

Typical man, Shannon thought. She bet he'd had a whole slew of attendants at his wedding. From the little he'd told her, his ex-wife had liked the finer things in life. Shannon briefly considered asking for details, then tamped the impulse down almost as quickly as it had surfaced.

Right now she couldn't handle thinking of Oliver marrying another woman.

As if sensing her turbulent mood, Oliver took her hand. With a single touch her world, which for the moment had tilted on its axis, righted itself.

Sounds of a Bach concerto filled the air as the cart drew to a smooth stop. When Oliver took out his wallet to tip, the driver shook his head. "We're being well compensated for our services. Enjoy the ceremony."

Oliver took her arm to steady her as she stepped from the vehicle in her heels.

"Oh, my" was all Shannon could manage to say when her gaze fell upon the elaborate stage.

Shannon expected a simple raised wooden platform large enough to hold four sets of brides and grooms and a minister. She hadn't expected something that looked as if it had been carved from stone and borrowed from the Parthenon. Four fluted Ionic columns formed a semicircle, topped with an ornate frieze containing four vertically channeled tablets depicting hearts.

Two steps led to the stone platform. Four tall urns filled to overflowing with gypsophila and delphinium were strategically positioned on the stage. The heavy mass of the white flowers was accentuated by deep red roses.

In the center aisle leading to the "temple," a white tapestry had been placed, flanked by red rose petals. White wooden chairs lined both sides of the center aisle. The ends of each row held bouquets of roses and greenery.

"This is more elaborate than I imagined." Though there was no need to speak softly, Shannon spoke in a hushed whisper.

"It's a Fortune wedding." Oliver responded with a chuckle. "Prepare to be impressed."

Chapter Twelve

As the lovely strains of another piece of classical music from the string quartet filled the air, Shannon's eyes turned dreamy. "I take back what I said about not wanting to share my day with three other brides. If I could have this, I'd happily share the day with a dozen others."

Though Oliver could see how Shannon might be awed by the sumptuous arrangements, he thought how it paled compared with his wedding at Saint Paul's Cathedral.

Diane had wanted a formal, elegant affair, complete with trumpets and royalty in attendance. But the marriage that was supposed to last a lifetime had barely made it to the three-year mark. Diane bore her share of the burden for the failure, but he now realized that he did, too.

"Oliver."

His name, said in that cultured British accent, had him banishing any thoughts of the past and smiling even before he turned. "Brodie."

Though normally too much of a buttoned-up Londoner for public displays of affection, Brodie Fortune Hayes surprised Oliver by giving him a manly half hug with a thump on the back.

"Good to see you." His brother glanced around. "Where's the little guy?"

"Ollie is with a baby minder for the evening. A couple I trust."

"Undoubtedly." Brodie's gaze slid away to settle on Shannon.

"Brodie Fortune Hayes, I'd like to introduce Miss Shannon Singleton. Shannon is a friend. She's also graciously consented to help me out by serving as Ollie's nanny while I'm in Horseback Hollow."

"Miss Singleton." Brodie extended his hand.

"Shannon, please." She smiled and shook his hand. "I knew you were brothers the moment I saw you."

At six feet tall, both men were the same height, with brown hair and vivid blue eyes. Like Oliver, his brother was dressed in a hand-tailored dark suit. Though, in Shannon's estimation, Oliver was the more handsome of the two.

If Rachel thought Oliver was a true Brit, Shannon couldn't wait until her friend got a load of Brodie. The man gave new meaning to the term "stiff upper lip."

"If you're not sitting with anyone, perhaps you'd like to sit with us," she offered.

Brodie's brow shot up and his gaze shifted to Oliver.

Shannon felt herself color. She hadn't meant to imply she and Oliver were a couple. The question now was how to backtrack without making everything worse.

Oliver didn't seem to notice the faux pas. "Yes, Brodie, you must sit with us."

"You two are...together?" Brodie spoke cautiously, as if feeling his way through a minefield.

"Has the transatlantic flight addled your brain?" Oliver spoke with more than a hint of exasperation. "Shannon is standing right here. I just introduced her to you. Of course we're together."

Brodie let the subject drop, though Shannon was aware of his speculative gaze as an usher took her arm to escort her to their seats.

She was amazed how close to the front they were seated until she realized that, of course, they'd be near the front. Oliver and Brodie's cousins were being married today.

Shannon had to admit she'd grown so used to chatting with Oliver that it was difficult to stay silent. But, as they waited for the ceremony to begin, she bit her tongue each time she was tempted to share an observation or impression.

It had been a while since Oliver had seen his brother. She wanted to give him a chance to speak with Brodie without having her in the middle of the conversation.

As guests continued to be seated, Shannon struck up a conversation with Cisco Mendoza, one of Gabi's brothers, who was seated to her right. He was a handsome man with dark hair and eyes, and a charming smile.

She was laughing at something Cisco said when Oliver touched her hand.

"The processional is ready to begin," he said in a low tone for her ears only.

Feeling as if she'd been caught doing something wrong—though she wasn't sure what it was—Shannon shifted her attention.

The bridesmaids moved slowly down the aisle, in dresses ranging from deep wine to seashell pink. Shannon wondered if Oliver noticed the color of the groomsmen's boutonnieres matched the respective bridesmaids' dress color.

Soon it was time for the maids of honor and best men to make their trek down the aisle. When they reached the stage, little MaryAnne Mendoza appeared holding a white wicker basket filled with rose petals of every hue. The three-year-old waved to people she knew and flung the petals with great gusto on her way to the platform, making more than a few in the audience chuckle.

Finally, the audience rose and one by one the four brides began their walk down the aisle on their fathers' arms. Shannon thought Gabi's father, Orlando, looked incredibly handsome in his dark suit. Oliver's mother, Josephine, must have thought so too, because Shannon caught her giving the handsome Latino a second glance.

"They're all so lovely," Shannon whispered to Oliver as the last bride joined her groom at the front.

Oliver simply smiled and squeezed her arm as they took their seats.

Considering there were four brides and four grooms to keep track of, everything proceeded seamlessly. Shannon found herself especially moved by the minister's sermon. He urged the couples to continue to nurture the love they now shared and to move from a "me first" attitude to "us first."

The ceremony continued with the lighting of the unity candle. The recitation of vows made Shannon sigh. Each set was so very personal and unique to the couple saying them. Love wove through the vows like a pretty ribbon, bringing a lump to Shannon's throat and a tear to her eyes.

Soon the radiant brides and grooms were making their way down the aisle. Shannon had no doubt each couple would enjoy the blessing of a happy marriage.

As thrilled as she was for all of them, Shannon couldn't stop a stab of envy as she wondered if she'd ever find such happiness.

If she did, one thing was certain, it wouldn't be with Oliver. In a matter of weeks, he'd be back in London. The thought was a dark cloud on the sunny day.

It didn't help that Shannon felt like a third wheel strolling with Brodie and Oliver to the barn for the dinner buffet and dance. It was obvious—to her at least—that Brodie was puzzled by her presence, probably wondering why she was intruding on his time with his brother.

Catching sight of Rachel, Shannon seized the out. She tapped Oliver's arm. "I need to speak with Rach. I'll catch you later."

She ignored his puzzled expression and shifted her gaze to Brodie. "It was a pleasure meeting you. I hope you enjoy your stay in Horseback Hollow."

Then she was gone, disappearing into the crowd.

Oliver couldn't stanch a surge of irritation. It wasn't as if he expected Shannon to spend every moment of the reception with him. Though he *had* given her a ride and stepped up to be her escort when she'd been left high and dry by her friend Rachel. The same friend she was now scurrying off to meet.

"Your nanny is very attractive," Brodie said in a slightly bored tone.

"She's not my nanny—she's Ollie's nanny," Oliver snapped.

"No need to get testy." Brodie narrowed his gaze. "Are you falling for the cowgirl?"

"She's an employee," Oliver said pointedly.

"So, you wouldn't mind if I got something going?" Brodie raised a brow. "A quick shag might make my brief stay in this backwoods town more palatable."

Oliver rounded on his brother, barely resisted the urge to grab him by the lapels of his Hugo Boss suit coat. "Stay away from her, Brodie. Shannon is off-limits. Understand?"

Brodie merely laughed. "I knew you had a thing for her."

"What are you talking about? I've already told you she's my—"

"Employee. I heard that part. But I have eyes. I see how you look at her. When she was talking with that man on the other side of her, you looked as if you wanted to punch him."

"I'm merely concerned about my employee's welfare." Oliver's penetrating gaze dared his brother to disagree.

"Whatever you say." As they entered the barn, Brodie's cynical look eased. "Whoever was in charge put a lot of time and money into planning this reception. It might be tolerable."

This time it was Oliver's turn to laugh. "It's good to have you here, Brodie. Let's get a glass of champagne."

The reception was in full swing, the dance floor was crowded and Shannon still hadn't crossed paths with Oliver. But she'd connected with almost everyone else in the entire county.

She'd even done her part by helping Gabi's four brothers, Matteo, Cisco, Alejandro and Joaquin, feel welcome by introducing them to all the single women she knew.

They were a good-looking bunch who had all the women swooning. Moments earlier she'd been leaving the dance floor with Cisco when they'd run into Delaney

Fortune. She'd introduced the two, then hurriedly excused herself. She'd promised Galen Fortune the next dance.

She'd known Galen since childhood. He was her buddy. Because there was only friendship between them, spending time with him was always easy and comfortable.

"You're a good dancer," she told Galen. "How is it that I didn't know that about you?"

He maneuvered her around the crowded dance floor with quick, sure steps. "Another one of my many hidden talents."

Shannon smiled and caught sight of Oliver speaking with his mother at the edge of the dance floor. She waved but he disappeared from view when Galen spun her around.

"It's kind of weird, isn't it?" Shannon said, relaxing in his arms.

"What is?"

Her lips twisted in a wry smile. "Being single when everyone around you is getting married."

Galen's brows pulled together. "Some just aren't lucky enough to find the right person. Me, I'd rather stay single than settle."

"Me, too," Shannon said, relieved to hear she wasn't the only one who felt that way. "I can't imagine anything worse than—"

"May I cut in?"

A thrill ran down Shannon's spine. Oliver wanted to dance with her.

Galen stepped back. "Thanks for the dance, Shannon."

She smiled warmly at him. "Any time."

Before she could catch her breath, she was in Oliver's arms. She loved the way he smelled, a woodsy mixture of cologne and soap and maleness that had heat percolating low in her belly. She let the intoxicating scent wrap around her.

"You two looked quite friendly."

"Galen? We're buddies from way back."

"Did you ever date?"

"No." Shannon laughed. "He's like another brother."

Was it only her imagination, or did Oliver's shoulders relax slightly?

"Have you enjoyed the festivities?" he asked.

"It's been fun. I've danced a lot."

"I noticed. You seemed to have developed a particular affinity for Gabi's brothers."

"They're nice guys." She lowered her voice. "The women all think they're incredibly hot."

He stared at her for a long moment. "What about you?"

She wasn't sure what made her be so bold, but she let her fingers caress his neck. "Let's just say I prefer a different type of man."

His eyes darkened to stormy pools of blue and he surprised them both when his hand flattened against her lower back, drawing her up against the length of his body.

He held her so close she could feel the evidence of his desire against her belly. The hardness ignited the flame that had been simmering inside her for days.

Slow it down, she told herself. It might simply be the romance in the air that was causing him to react to her this way.

But she had to admit, whatever the reason, she liked having him stare at her with such blatant hunger in his gaze.

"My brother thinks you're hot," he murmured, twining strands of her hair loosely around his fingers.

It took Shannon a second to find her voice. "He—he's not my type, either."

"Who is your type, Shannon?" he asked in a husky voice.

There was a beat of silence. "I believe you know the answer to that question, Oliver."

Even as his mouth relaxed into a slight smile, he tightened his hold.

Shannon sighed with pure pleasure. Dancing with Oliver, being held so firmly in his strong, capable arms, was all she wanted, all she needed. Forget Galen and Brodie. Forget the Mendoza brothers.

Forget our agreement.

Shannon opened her mouth to tell him she'd been wrong to insist things stay strictly business. But as they dipped and swayed to the romantic melody, she found it impossible to think, much less speak. The world around her disappeared and all she knew was they fit together perfectly and she was right where she wanted to be…

Reluctant to give up the intimacy, she lost herself in the music, drifting on a cloud of pure pleasure until the jarring ring of his cell phone shattered the moment.

Shannon lifted her head as he slipped the phone from his pocket and glanced at the readout.

"Working on a Saturday night?" she teased.

"It's your parents' number."

Her breath caught, then began again. They wouldn't call unless it was important. A jolt of uneasiness went through her.

Oliver pressed the phone against his ear and talked with her mother as he maneuvered them to the far edge of the dance floor, where it wasn't so noisy.

"How high?" His mouth tightened into a grim line. "I'll be right there."

"What's wrong?"

Shadows played in his eyes, making them unreadable. "Ollie has a fever. One hundred and three." His brows knit together as he calculated. "Thirty-nine point four Celsius."

"Fevers that high aren't uncommon in a child his age."

"I can't stay." His gaze darted to the exit. "I can have one of my family members take you home."

"No need." Shannon snatched her bag up from the table where she'd left it earlier. "I'm going with you."

Chapter Thirteen

Oliver unbuckled Ollie from the car seat and carried him into the house, his strides so long and quick that Shannon had to run to keep pace. Once inside, he flipped on the lights with one hand and sat the boy down on the sofa. Barnaby immediately jumped up to sit beside him.

"Let the dog be," she told Oliver when his arm moved to swipe the animal off the sofa.

Confusion turned to understanding when the boy wrapped his arms around the corgi, resting his head against the dog's soft fur.

"I'll get the thermometer so we can recheck his temperature," Shannon told Oliver. Thankfully, after a recent trip to the store, she'd stocked the medicine chest in the bathroom with all the necessities. "Mom gave him some acetaminophen before we got there so it should start coming down."

"Stop," Oliver ordered, pushing up from the sofa. "You sit here with Ollie. He needs someone to comfort him."

Shannon moved to the sofa. She didn't argue, though she could make a good case that it should be his daddy comforting him rather than a relatively new nanny. But Ollie had taken to her from the start and now, even as she took Oliver's spot on the sofa, the child cuddled against her.

In less than a minute, Oliver returned with the temporal scanner. Shannon talked him through how to use it. A lethargic Ollie only whimpered.

Some of the grimness around Oliver's mouth eased at the readout. "One hundred and one."

Shannon exhaled the breath she didn't realize she'd been holding. "Better."

She brushed Ollie's hair back from his face and Barnaby licked her hand. The boy's eyes were closed now and his respirations were easy and regular.

"He's asleep," Shannon spoke softly, her voice barely above a whisper. She glanced up at Oliver. "Think we should try to put him in the crib?"

"Let's give it a few more minutes." Oliver sat on the other side of Ollie and the dog. His gaze lingered on her dress, a bunch of lace clutched between Ollie's fingers. "You can take my car if you'd like to return to the reception."

"Are you crazy? I'm not leaving Ollie."

Or you, she thought. His son's unexpected fever had clearly shaken Oliver.

Shannon brushed back a lock of Ollie's soft brown hair. Tears stung the backs of her eyes. Oliver wasn't the only one who'd been shaken. With his eyes closed and his skin so pale, Ollie looked so little, so defenseless.

"Children are such a responsibility," Oliver said quietly as he gazed at his sleeping child.

"And such a joy." Her heart rose to her throat. Shannon

realized she wasn't halfway in love with Ollie. She was totally in love with the little guy.

"You like children." Oliver's gaze never left hers. "The first time I saw you interact with him, I knew."

She nodded, feeling oddly embarrassed by the blatant admiration in his eyes.

"I've always loved children," she admitted. "Do you know when I was a little girl, I told my parents I wanted half a dozen kids when I grew up? Truth is, I'd still like a whole houseful."

As she'd hoped, the statement distracted Oliver from his worry. His eyes widened. "Seriously?"

"Yep." Shannon gave a little laugh, then lowered her voice to a confidential whisper. "Let's keep that our secret. Something like that gets out and any potential suitors will run screaming away into the night, never to be seen again."

He gave her a dubious glance. "You're kidding."

"I wish I were. Let me give you an example." Shannon shifted slightly and repositioned Ollie in her lap. "I dated this guy when I lived in Lubbock. We had fun together. Things were going well, until the subject of children came up. One night I said to him what I just said to you. You'd have thought I'd exploded a grenade under him."

Oliver cocked his head, his eyes bright with interest.

"His reaction made more sense when he told me he wasn't sure he even wanted kids…ever." Shannon expelled a breath and shook her head. "He called me once after that, but it was over. Now, if a guy asks, I just say I like children and hope to have a couple someday."

Oliver rubbed his chin. "Why not be honest?"

"I am being honest. I do like children. I do hope to have a couple. But having more would need to be something my husband wanted, too." Shannon gave a little laugh. "I have my doubts that I'll find any man who wants six."

"My mother had six," Oliver reminded her.

"Mine had five," Shannon said. "But I think things were different back then. Big families were more the norm."

"I don't know how they did it." Oliver glanced at his son. "Being a parent is exhausting."

"You even have household help," she pointed out.

"It's not only the physical care," Oliver said, almost to himself. "I'm organized and disciplined. Though I certainly don't know how I'd do it without a nanny and a housekeeper. But…"

He paused for a long moment then continued.

"Being a parent makes me feel vulnerable in ways I don't particularly like." His gaze lingered on his son. She saw the love in his eyes…and the fear. "I never thought I was capable of loving so deeply. It would kill me to lose him."

How had she ever thought Oliver was a cold fish or that Ollie was simply an obligation?

"That's the downside of caring for someone," Shannon said solemnly. "It makes you vulnerable. My grandmother used to say love isn't for the faint of heart."

She wasn't sure how the phrase translated into Brit-speak, but from the look that crossed his face he got the gist.

"It can be frightening to have such intense feelings." Oliver raked a hand through his hair. "Especially when you aren't certain if the other person feels the same way."

Shannon was fully prepared to tell him Ollie wouldn't go to him so easily or let himself be comforted if there wasn't love and trust between them.

Then Shannon realized his gaze wasn't on his son, but on *her*. It wasn't Ollie's feelings he was wondering about, but hers. The knowledge gave her a subtle, pleasurable jolt.

She dropped her gaze to the boy, feeling warmth rise up her neck. "I think we can put him to bed now."

"Let me." Oliver rose, then bent over and carefully lifted his son from the sofa.

A second later, Barnaby hopped off the sofa, hitting the floor with a thud.

"While you get Ollie settled," Shannon said in a low tone, "I'll take Barnaby outside."

Oliver's brows drew together. "Stay close to the house and in the light. I heard howling out there."

"Coyotes." Her tone was matter-of-fact. The animals were a fact of life in the area. "They normally don't venture close to the house, especially when the floodlights are on."

"C'mon, Barnaby." She started toward the door, the dog padding behind her.

"Shannon."

She turned, raised a brow.

"Wait a minute. Once I get Ollie settled, we can take Barnaby out together."

"Sure. That'll work." Shannon didn't mind waiting.

Not because she was some wussy who couldn't stand being in the dark by herself, or because she was fearful of a few coyotes. But because it'd be nice to have the company. Especially on such a beautiful night when the moon was full and a plethora of stars filled the clear night sky.

Instead of remaining in the living room, Shannon followed Oliver into Ollie's room. She turned on the Mickey Mouse night-light and removed the stuffed animals from the crib.

Oliver laid the boy down, removing his jeans, shoes and socks with now well-practiced movements, leaving the child clad only in a T-shirt and diaper.

After checking the diaper, Oliver looked up. "Dry."

"Good. I know my mom said she'd changed him right before we got there, but still—"

"A soggy nappy would have awakened him for sure."

"Right. And what he needs right now is uninterrupted rest." After checking his temperature one last time, Oliver motioned Shannon out of the room.

"It's down another degree," Oliver confided, relief etched on his face.

"Good." Shannon squeezed his hand.

After they were a safe distance down the hall, Shannon turned to the dog. "It's time, Barnaby. Let's go outside."

The dog emitted a low woof and sped to the back door, his short legs moving surprisingly fast.

But speed disappeared once Barnaby was outside. The corgi took his time sniffing every bush and tree in the area. Though the night air had a bit of a bite, Shannon wasn't cold. Oliver stood beside her on the bricked patio and heat rolled off him in waves.

"I want to kiss you," he surprised her by saying as the silence lengthened.

Her stomach felt as if it had dropped three feet straight down.

"Then why don't you?" Even though her heart raced wildly, she spoke in the same matter-of-fact tone he'd used.

Oliver studied her for several seconds before he spoke, his steady gaze shooting tingles down her spine. "We have an agreement."

"I release you from that agreement," she said in a solemn tone. If she'd had a magic wand, she'd have tapped his shoulder for good measure.

Oliver shook his head. "You're still my employee."

Her heartbeat hitched. "I'm not."

"Unfortunately you are." He expelled a heavy breath but didn't take a step away. Instead Oliver moved closer.

Shannon recognized the signs. He was waiting, hoping, for her to convince him. Lifting her chin, she shook her head slowly from side to side, a tiny smile lifting the corners of her mouth. "You may be the one who signs my paycheck, but actually I work for Ollie."

For a second those blue eyes were simply astonished. "Ollie is a child. You can't work for him."

"I beg to differ." Her voice had taken on a playful edge. "He's my focus. So, technically I work for him."

"Let's say I accept that premise, which by the way is quite a stretch of logic. It doesn't negate the fact that if we begin an affair…"

Shannon held herself very still, firmly ignoring the unsettling flutter his words caused in her midsection.

"I thought we were talking about a kiss," she said with a studied nonchalance that deserved an acting award.

The look he shot her fried every brain cell she possessed, and then some. "We both know where one kiss will lead."

Yes, and Shannon wanted him so desperately it was a wonder she hadn't ripped his clothes off before now.

Not sure of the steadiness of her voice, Shannon settled for a jerky nod.

"This—" He paused, as if searching for the words. "Whatever happens would be a temporary thing."

Her heart performed another series of flutters. When she opened her mouth to say she didn't care, to say—

"I'm not looking for a relationship." She saw a flicker of challenge in his eyes. "And I won't be in Horseback Hollow that much longer."

Even with shadows playing in his eyes, making them difficult to read, she swore she saw regret lurking there. Nonetheless, his words were clear. He'd spelled it out, leaving no room for fanciful thoughts of happily-ever-after.

Though Shannon had grown up in a traditional home and had been taught intimacy was only coupled with love, and then only after marriage, this was her life and her decision.

She cared deeply for Oliver, she respected him and she was physically attracted to him in a major way. What would be the harm in stealing some moments of pleasure? Especially if they both went into an affair with eyes wide open.

Apparently misunderstanding her hesitation, Oliver reached over and squeezed her hand. His voice was soft, reaching inside her to a raw, tender place. "Refraining is the wisest course of action."

Yet, at his simple touch, sensation licked up her arm, down her breasts and on down to pool between her thighs. Heat simmered in the night air.

When he started to pull his hand back, she brought it to her mouth and placed a kiss in the palm. "Depends I guess on your definition of *wise*."

His blue eyes darkened. "What are you saying?"

The intoxicating scent of his cologne wrapped around her senses. Her gaze met his.

"I'm saying I want you." Her eyes searched his. "I'm okay with it not being forever. I'm not sure I'm ready for forever, anyway."

"I don't want to hurt you."

She gave a little laugh, her pulse a swift, tripping beat. "Uh, correct me if I'm wrong. I believe it's pleasure—not pain—on tap tonight."

Still, he made no move toward her. "Are you sure?"

Shannon took a step closer, wound her arms around him and planted a kiss at the base of his neck, his skin salty beneath her lips. Then she lifted her face, and met his dark gaze with what she hoped was a sexy smile. "Very sure."

"Well, then…" He folded her more fully into his arms, anchoring her against his chest as his mouth covered hers in a deep, compelling kiss.

He continued to kiss her with a slow thoroughness that left her weak, trembling and longing for more. When his tongue swept across her lips seeking access, she eagerly opened her mouth to him, her tongue fencing with his.

The warmth in her lower belly turned fiery hot and became a pulsating need.

Barnaby's deep woof barely registered.

Another bark and the dog sprang. The unexpected impact of the solid body against the back of her knee knocked Shannon off balance. Only Oliver's strong arms saved her from a tumble.

"Barnaby." She dropped her gaze to the dog, who now sat at her feet. "What is your problem?"

"He's ready to go inside." Oliver's mouth skimmed the edge of her jaw. "It's a good plan."

Keeping a firm grip on her arm, Oliver opened the sliding glass door. The dog bounded inside, nails clattering against the hardwood, and made a beeline for Ollie's room.

With her fingers linked with Oliver's, Shannon followed the dog down the hallway. When Barnaby plopped down on the rug next to the crib, Shannon stepped around him to lean over the rail.

Oliver joined her.

"His cheeks aren't flushed anymore," he said, his voice filled with relief.

Shannon placed the back of her hand on Ollie's forehead. "His skin is cool."

She and Oliver exchanged a smile, then eased silently from the room. They stood in the hall and Shannon fought against a sudden wave of awkwardness and uncertainty. "I don't know about you, but I'm ready for bed."

"You took the words out of my mouth."

She tilted her head back, met his gaze. She'd never seen such beautiful eyes. Or such compelling eyes. Or eyes that had a weakening effect on her knees.

Oliver reached out and touched her cheek, one finger trailing slowly along her skin until it reached the line of her jaw. "I can't wait to have you in my bed."

Then, before she even had a second to breathe, his lips were on hers, exquisitely gentle and achingly tender. He took the fingers of her hand and kissed them, featherlight. "Unless you've changed your mind?"

"Race you there," she said and, with a breathless laugh, started to run.

Chapter Fourteen

Oliver caught up with Shannon just as she reached the doorway. She giggled like a giddy teenager when he spun her around.

"Caught you," he said.

"I let you catch me." How was it that standing here, both of them grinning like two fools, felt so right?

She'd had two other love affairs, one in college and one when she lived in Lubbock. While in both cases she'd had high hopes for a future with the guy, being with them had never felt quite right.

Now, here she stood beside a man who'd made it clear whatever they shared would be very short-term, and she had no hesitation or doubts.

Like now, having him scatter kisses down her neck felt natural and oh-so right.

"Hmm." Shannon tilted her head back, giving him full access to the creamy expanse of skin. "I love the feel of your arms around me."

"I love the taste of you." His lips continued their down-ward journey. Only when he reached the vee of her dress did he lift his head. "This dress drives me absolutely bonkers."

She gave a pleased laugh. For that one compliment alone, the dress had been worth every penny she'd spent. "Oh, so it's the dress you fancy, is it?"

Oliver chuckled, then kicked the bedroom door shut with his foot, reaching around her to lock it. "I fancy every part of you."

The sentiment, coupled with the wicked look in his dancing blue eyes, sent warmth sliding through her veins like warm honey.

"Locking the door seems a bit excessive," she said, her tone light and teasing. "Concerned about Barnaby doing some spying?"

"I don't want anything to disturb us," he said, then his smile turned rueful. "Except—"

Shannon didn't know what to think when he abruptly released her and strode to the bedside stand. When she saw him flip on the baby monitor, her admiration for him inched up another notch.

"Just in case Ollie needs us." In several long strides he was back beside her, pulling her to him.

"I must admit I find your concern for Ollie—" she leaned close to whisper in his ear "—incredibly arousing."

"I'll remember that." His eyes twinkled. "All I ask is you do your best to restrain any carnal urges while I'm checking his temperature or changing his nappy."

Shannon realized she was seeing a playful side of Oliver that up until now she'd caught only glimpses of. "This relaxed, fun side of you is also sexy."

"I'm beginning to think," he said, brushing back a

strand of hair that had fallen across her cheek, "that everything about me turns you on."

Shannon pretended to think for a second, then grinned. "Pretty much."

"We're going to take our time tonight. No rushing allowed." His expression turned serious. "That will be difficult, considering I've wanted to kiss you for a very long time."

"Well, what are you waiting for?" She lifted her face to him and placed her hand on his chest, toying with a button. She slipped it open. "What do you say? Let's get this party started."

Shannon felt her knees grow weak at the fire in his eyes. An answering heat flared through her, a sensation she didn't bother to fight.

"Oliver." She spoke his name, then paused, not sure what she wanted to say. Her eyes, which seemed to suddenly develop a mind of their own, zeroed in on the area directly below his belt buckle.

He chuckled, a low pleasant rumbling sound.

"Slow," he murmured, twining strands of her hair loosely around his fingers the same way he had when they'd danced earlier, "means keeping our clothes on a little while longer."

Shannon stuck out her lip and pretended to pout. The effect was spoiled by the smile that kept forming on her mouth. "I don't like this game."

"Oh, but you will." His voice was like a promise.

Shannon lifted her gaze and their eye contact turned into something more, a tangible connection between the two of them. Could he hear her heart pounding? How could he not?

"You're pretty full of yourself, mister," she managed to sputter.

Oliver winked. "That's a Fortune for you."

Shannon's laughter disappeared when his hands spanned her waist. He ran his palms up along the sides of her dress, skimming the curve of her breast, and she forgot how to breathe.

Her nipples stiffened, straining against the fabric toward his touch.

"You are so lovely," he whispered into her ear right before he took the lobe between his teeth and nibbled.

Shivers rippled across her skin.

Without warning, he shifted and pressed his mouth against hers. When his tongue swept across her lips seeking access, Shannon eagerly opened her mouth to him, her tongue fencing with his.

He tasted like the most delicious decadent candy she'd ever eaten. And she couldn't help wanting more.

Still, as he promised, Oliver didn't rush. He simply continued to kiss her. Testosterone wafted from him like an invisible tether, tugging at Shannon, keeping her feet anchored to the floor and her mouth melded to his.

The feeling of his mouth on hers was like nothing Shannon had experienced before.

She ached for him, desired him, with her entire being. The need quickly became a stark carnal hunger she hadn't known she was even capable of feeling.

"I want—" she whispered against his mouth, when they came up for air "—you."

"I'm not going anywhere," he said, his voice a husky caress.

"I want you naked." In a display of unexpected boldness, she pushed her hips against him, rubbing his erection.

"I planned to take this slow," he reminded her, his breath hitching. "Savor every moment."

"Plans have changed," she said. "Next time we'll go slow. For now, get naked."

"Heaven protect me from a bossy woman." But his eyes glittered and his clothes quickly landed in a heap next to hers on the floor.

She'd been hot only seconds before, but now, when his gaze shifted to her naked body and lingered, Shannon felt exposed and vulnerable. She almost embarrassed herself by trying to cover her most private parts with her hands… until she saw the stark desire in his eyes. Desire…for her.

To realize he wanted her as much as she did him was a heady feeling and a confidence booster. Her hands remained at her sides.

"You are…magnificent." He breathed the words and took her hands loosely in his.

"You're not so bad yourself." An understatement, but the best Shannon could manage at the moment. Broad shoulders, hard chest, lean hips, Oliver Fortune Hayes was every woman's fantasy.

Though a businessman, Oliver had a workingman's body, corded with muscle, lean and tan. Dark hair converged on the flat planes of his stomach into a line that…

She inhaled sharply and her knees suddenly felt weak.

Without warning, he scooped her up and carried her to the bed.

"Hey," she laughingly protested, "what do you think you're doing?"

"Something tells me you're going to be at your best horizontal."

The bed was soft and luxurious, and the tiny part of her brain still capable of rational thought registered the fact that he must have had a new mattress delivered.

Rational thought disappeared as Oliver settled beside her and once again began to kiss her. Not slow and easy as he had before but with a voraciousness that showed a mounting hunger.

The same hunger that was rapidly consuming her.

She could have cheered when his thumbs brushed across the tight points of her nipples. His stroking fingers sent shock waves of pleasure through her body.

"Oh, Oli—"

Whatever she'd been about to say died away on a soft little whimper as he found one sensitive part of her body after another. His hands continued to move, to search; touching, stroking, caressing until her heart pounded and she didn't even know her own name. All Shannon knew was she needed him to continue touching her.

"Your breasts are perfect," he whispered. "I need to taste you. Open your eyes."

Shannon opened her eyes. As she watched, he touched the tip of his tongue to the tip of her right breast. The combination of seeing and feeling brought her up off the bed and had her crying out in delight.

He smiled, then circled her nipple with his tongue before drawing it fully into his mouth. The gentle sucking had her arching against him. At the same time, his hand slipped between her legs.

She parted for him, catching her breath as he rubbed against her slick center. Then his head was moving down to where his fingers still caressed, scattering kisses down her belly.

The tension filling her body continued to increase exponentially with each warm, moist kiss against her bare skin until she stiffened, realizing just where those wickedly clever lips were headed. Part of her suspected what Oliver was going to do while the rest of her couldn't believe it was really happening. She'd heard…she'd read… but she never had…

His openmouthed kiss between her legs had her writhing in pleasure. He found her sweet spot and licked it over and over again until all she could do was dig her heels into the mattress and clutch the sheets with her hands.

How could it be she'd lived this long and had never known such pleasure existed?

"I want you inside me," she said even as her muscles tensed and collected and her breath came in ragged pants.

She didn't have to ask twice.

Oliver pulled away briefly and she heard the sound of foil tearing. Then he was over her.

She reached between them and guided him inside.

He was large and stretched her in the best way possible. Her legs swept around his hips as he began to move slowly inside her in a rhythm as old as time.

Shannon felt filled, yet the need—that all-encompassing need for him—propelled her to want more. She clung to him, urging him deeper.

The rhythmic thrusting grew faster. As she surged against the pleasure swelling like the tide inside her, Shannon heard herself groan, a sound of want and need that astonished her with its intensity.

Her blood had become a fire in her veins, her pulse throbbing hard and thick.

Seconds later, the orgasm ripped through her, hitting with breathtaking speed. Her entire body convulsed then released.

As she cried out, Oliver caught her mouth in a hard kiss.

He continued to thrust until every last drop of pleasure had been wrung from her. Only then did he take his release, shuddering in her arms and calling out her name.

For a moment he simply lay there on top of her, a sweet heavy weight. When he rolled off, she murmured a protest.

In answer, his arm slipped around her, not confining,

but comfortable. With a contented sigh, Shannon snuggled against his chest and discovered her head fit perfectly just under his chin.

He was warm and solid. A man she could hold on to, a man she could count on. At least for another few weeks…

Shannon fought to keep her eyes open.

"You kept your promise," she murmured before she fell into a sated slumber. "It was so very good."

Oliver waited until Shannon's breathing had turned easy and deep before he slipped from her embrace to check on Ollie. Even after he confirmed his son's fever had remained down and the child was resting comfortably, he didn't return to bed.

Instead he headed to the kitchen and poured himself a glass of whiskey. Sipping from a tumbler shaped like a boot, he stared into the darkness.

He'd had sex with a number of women, but tonight had been different. Shannon had touched a part of him that Oliver had always kept well hidden. From the time Oliver had been a small boy, his father had taught him to guard his emotions. Although the man had never struck him, Rhys Henry Hayes's tongue had been a potent weapon; sharp as a knife and capable of drawing blood.

His father had been fond of saying he didn't tolerate fools. To Rhys's warped way of thinking, a fool was anyone who cared too much and let it show. That included little boys.

Taking another sip of whiskey, Oliver thought of the words Diane had flung in his face the day she moved out. She'd accused him of being as cold as his father and told him it was no wonder she had looked for love elsewhere.

At the time, he'd shrugged aside the arrow that had been aimed to wound, concluding it was her way of excusing her own poor behavior. Now he wondered if there might have been some truth to the statement. Still, something had kept him from fully trusting his wife, and in the end Diane's duplicity had shown his instincts had been spot-on.

Shannon, on the other hand, was a different story. It would be easy to let her get too close, and that would be disastrous for all concerned. She was a small-town girl who loved living close to family and friends. Her home was in Horseback Hollow. His home—his life—was in London.

Her mind, her heart, the person she was fascinated him. Her body tempted him. She was the total package, and that's what made her so hard to resist, both in bed and out. That's what would keep him coming back for more. He knew there was so much more of this fascinating woman left to plumb.

The thought made him smile, remembering all he'd plumbed tonight—

Arms slid around his bare chest. "I hope that smile means you're thinking about me."

When Oliver turned, he found Shannon wearing one of his shirts, hanging open save for a single button. Her hair was a tangled mass of curls and her gaze was sloe-eyed and sensual.

He flipped the button open, then eased back the shirt and let it slide to the floor. His mouth skimmed the edge of her jaw, testing the sweetness of her skin. "You must be a mind reader."

She laughed softly and wound her arms around his neck, lifting her face for a kiss.

Though it hadn't been all that long since he'd left her side, it felt amazingly good to hold her again. To taste her. To smell her. He spread his hands over her buttocks and pressed her against his erection.

"Well, hel-lo there," she said, her eyes teasing.

He bent his head and kissed her softly on the mouth. "I haven't had nearly enough of you."

"You stole the words right out of my mouth."

"I love your mouth." Once again his lips closed over hers.

She kissed him back, and the kisses quickly became more urgent and fevered. Then abruptly she stepped back, swaying slightly.

He reached out and took her arm, concern deepening his voice. "Problem?"

"Just a couple shaky knees that aren't going to hold me up much longer." She grasped his hand, tugging and gesturing with her head toward the bedroom. "Remember, I'm at my best horizontal."

Oliver chuckled. Locking his hand around her elbow in a secure grip, he propelled her into the bedroom. Once the door was shut and locked, they tumbled onto the bed.

Though his body responded with breathtaking speed, this time, he took it slow. He wanted it to be perfect for her.

When the last shudder had left her body and she lay spent beneath him, Oliver held her close and savored the moment.

Still, his last thought before he joined her in sleep was that he had to keep up his guard. It would be far too easy to pretend he never had to let her go and start to believe this was exactly where he belonged.

Chapter Fifteen

Oliver pulled the rental car into the long driveway and mentally calculated the hours until he'd be able to leave. He couldn't use the excuse that their baby minder wanted them home early. Ollie was spending the night with Oliver's aunt Jeanne Marie.

Though he'd hoped to spend some quality time with his mother this weekend, Oliver never imagined it would involve attending something called a "card party" on a Saturday night. Especially a party held at the home of Shannon's parents.

The monthly event had been rescheduled from last weekend. Apparently too many of the "regulars" had wanted to attend the Fortune weddings, so they'd voted to move the card party back a week.

Oliver hadn't seen Shep or Lilian since the night of the wedding. Which meant he hadn't had to look in Shep Singleton's face since he'd begun shagging his daughter.

Though initially Oliver had told himself that what had happened after the wedding had been a one-time—okay, a two-time—thing, it had seemed so natural to go to her the next day. By Wednesday, a romp between the sheets had become a daily affair.

Of course, because of his crazy work hours, any love-making had to occur before midnight or after lunch. So far that hadn't been an issue. When he wanted something, he was pretty adept at making it happen.

And Oliver wanted Shannon Singleton. He wanted her with an intensity that continued to amaze him. It wasn't just physical. Shannon made him laugh and feel things he hadn't let himself feel in years.

Like with Ollie. Oliver hadn't realized it until she'd casually mentioned that she'd noticed he never told his son that he loved him.

"It goes without saying," he said, recalling his exact words. "I take care of him. I work hard to put food on the table and give him what he needs."

"He needs to hear the words," she'd insisted.

When he hesitated, she'd taken his hand and marched him into the living room, where Ollie had sat playing with his bricks.

"Tell him," she urged in a low voice.

Feeling incredibly silly, Oliver had crouched down beside his son. He opened his mouth, then closed it and cleared his throat. Why did something that should have been so easy come so hard to him?

"Ollie."

The boy looked up, his smile wide. He held up an *A* brick for Oliver to admire. "See."

"It's very nice." If Oliver had been alone, he'd have simply patted the boy on the head and stood up.

But Shannon stood there, looking at him with such

encouragement—and confidence—he couldn't back down. Not even with his father's words rolling around in his head.

It really wasn't a big thing, he told himself, just three little words. People said them all the time, even if they didn't mean them. But Oliver would mean them. He loved Ollie, more than he'd ever thought possible.

Just. Say. The. Words.

"Ollie." He gently touched the little boy's face and gazed into his eyes. "I love you."

The boy's smile was like a flash of sunshine warming everything it touched, thawing out a part of his heart that had been frozen for too long. Though Oliver was fairly certain the toddler hadn't understood what he said, Shannon had been right. He'd needed to say the words.

Oliver scrubbed the boy's head with his hand and then stood.

"Go ahead and play with your bricks." His voice had been thick with emotion and had shaken slightly. He'd felt foolish and more than a little angry that he couldn't seem to control the intense feelings welling up inside him.

Then Shannon had wrapped her arms around him and given him a big kiss. When she'd stepped back, the pride in her eyes washed away everything but joy.

"Earth to Oliver." Shannon's voice broke through his thoughts. "I think we should go inside."

Oliver pulled his thoughts back to the present. "I'm not looking forward to this evening."

"The fact that you pulled up and have yet to turn off the engine tells me you're still considering making a break for it."

She knew him so well. Why did he find the thought so disturbing?

"Forgive me if I don't want to spend a Saturday playing cards with my mother." His tone was curter than he'd intended.

Her cheery smile faded and she stiffened. "If you didn't want to come, you shouldn't have accepted the invitation."

"It's not just that," he reluctantly admitted.

"What then?"

"It's your father."

"My dad?" Her eyes widened then narrowed. "What has he done now?"

"I told him I wouldn't touch you when—"

"You've been doing nothing but touching me for the past week and in every possible place."

Just the words said in that throaty whisper had him going hard. He shifted uncomfortably in his seat.

"I'd promised him he had nothing to worry about." Oliver set his jaw in a hard tilt. "I assured him you would be totally safe living under my roof."

"I am safe living under your roof." Shannon reached over and wrapped her fingers around his hand.

The simple touch eased a little of the tension that held him in a stranglehold.

"You would never let anything bad happen to me. If someone broke in, you'd protect me. If I hurt myself, you'd tend to me." Her voice was low and soothing. "I *am* safe. The sex, well, that's something private between you and me."

Oliver frowned, realizing he didn't like hearing her refer to what they shared as *sex*. *Shagging* also didn't fit.

But that left *lovemaking*, and that didn't work either. There was warmth, there was caring, but love wasn't part of the equation.

"My father will never suspect," she assured him.

But halfway through the evening, when they were between games and Oliver had unconsciously slid his arm around Shannon's waist and she'd leaned into him, the look in Shep's eyes could have cut steel.

Oliver should have known better than to get too close to Shannon. Though he'd never been a demonstrative kind of man, she was very much the opposite. She was always finding excuses to touch him, and he'd discovered he liked it.

He'd also seen how it pleasured her when he unexpectedly reached over and took her hand or gave her a hug when she came in the door. It had seemed such a little thing to do to make her happy.

He'd also been more demonstrative with Ollie, and the boy had become more openly loving with him. Yesterday his son had even called him "Daddy" for the first time. Just recalling the moment brought a lump to his throat.

"When will you be leaving our little town, Oliver?" Shep asked pointedly during a brief conversational lull.

"Oh, Shep, must you bring up such a disturbing topic?" Josephine's brows knit together in a frown. "It feels as if Oliver and Ollie just got here, and now you're bringing up their departure."

"Can't ignore the facts." Shep took a swig of beer straight from the bottle. "Thought I heard you'll be returning to London in just a couple of weeks."

Beneath his arm, Oliver felt Shannon stiffen. They'd agreed not to talk about when he would leave, and Oliver inwardly cursed Shep for bringing up the topic. But the man's comment required an answer.

"Not that soon." Oliver kept his tone easy. "Closer to the end of March."

"Several weeks then, but not that long off." Shep shot a pointed look in his daughter's direction, as if making sure she was listening, before his gaze returned to Oliver. "You have a girl back home?"

"Pardon?"

"A girl. A woman you're seeing."

"No," Oliver said coolly.

"My son has been much too busy the past year to do much socializing," Josephine interjected. "His brokerage firm keeps him extremely busy, and now that he has Ollie to care for, I doubt there'll be much time for dating."

"Oh, I'm sure he'll find a few free moments now and then." Shep took another swig of beer. "Your son seems like the type to take advantage of every opportunity."

Oliver heard Shannon's quick intake of breath. If they'd been alone, Oliver would have had no hesitation in calling Shep on his comment. But the rest of those in attendance seemed oblivious to the conversation's undertones.

To make a scene would serve no purpose, he told himself even as his spine stiffened.

Oliver met Shep's gaze. They would talk, his eyes told her father, soon.

"Did I tell you Ollie has now started calling Oliver 'Daddy'?" This time it was Shannon who filled the silence. "It's so cute. He clearly says 'Daddy,' not 'Dada.'"

"Shannon called Shep 'Da' until she was three."

Shannon gave a little laugh. "Oh, Mother."

Lilian lifted her hand as if swearing an oath. "True story."

"Tell them what the boy calls you," Shep said to Shannon.

The slight pink across her cheeks deepened, but she acted as if she hadn't heard.

Josephine took a sip of tea, considered. "I believe 'Shannon' would be difficult for a child to say."

Shep opened his mouth.

"He calls me 'Mama,'" Shannon said, then quickly added, "I think it's what he calls all females."

"He calls your mother 'Lil,'" her dad said.

A lightning bolt flashed in Shannon's eyes. Oliver

couldn't believe her own father hadn't noticed his daughter's mounting irritation. Perhaps Shep didn't care. Perhaps he wanted to get a rise out of her.

Or perhaps this was his way of making a point. Steer clear of Oliver Fortune Hayes. He'll eat you up and spit you out and never look back.

Shannon pushed to her feet and flashed a smile that didn't quite reach her eyes.

"I'm really tired. Ollie was up a lot last night." She slanted a glance at Oliver. "I hope you don't mind leaving early."

"Not at all. It's embarrassing when your own mum trounces you." Oliver bent over and brushed a kiss against his mother's cheek. "May we give you a ride home?"

Josephine smiled and glanced over at Orlando Mendoza, who'd been her partner most of the evening. "Thank you, but I believe I have that covered."

Oliver and Shannon made their exit in record time. Once they were in the car, Shannon rested her head against the back of the seat and huffed a frustrated breath.

"My father was in rare form tonight." Her lips tightened. "No doubt about it. He's figured out we're sleeping together."

There was no reason to disagree. That fact had been very obvious. "You're his little girl. He's concerned I'm going to hurt you."

"I'm a woman, not a child," she snapped. "We both went into this with our eyes wide open."

Oliver didn't want to ask, but knew the question would fester if he didn't. "Any regrets?"

The anger fled her eyes, replaced with another kind of heat. She leaned over and brushed a kiss against his cheek. "Only that we're not at home right now so I can have my way with you."

* * *

The next week passed swiftly. Shannon kept her days so full she didn't have time to think. It was at night, when Ollie was in bed and Oliver was working, that her mind raced and she did nothing but think.

She thought about the fact that the Fortune Foundation would soon be choosing its new marketing executive. What would she do if the foundation offered the position to Rachel and not her? She couldn't continue to stay in Horseback Hollow and simply help out around the ranch. But the thought of returning to Lubbock filled her with dread.

But what weighed most heavily on her mind was the knowledge that each passing day brought her closer to the time when Oliver and Ollie would leave her and return to England.

Barely aware of the fragrant aroma of vegetables and meat cooking in the pot before her, Shannon automatically stirred the soup and blinked back tears.

This time spent with Oliver and Ollie had been the best of her life. Living under the same roof with Oliver had given her extra insight into the man behind the British stiff upper lip. He wasn't cold and off-putting as Rachel thought. He was a warm, caring man with a huge capacity for love.

At her encouragement, Oliver had become more demonstrative with Ollie. The increased openness was already bearing fruit. Ollie now ran to his father as often as he ran to her. And just yesterday, when Ollie had fallen on the rocky driveway and skinned his knee, his father had been the one he wanted to comfort him.

Oh, how she was going to miss them both. Shannon sighed and picked up the spoon.

She started to stir the soup again and felt a tug at her pant leg.

"Mama, up." Ollie stood beside her, arms held high.

Setting the spoon down, she lowered the heat even more, then stepped back and lifted the boy into her arms.

He smelled like soap and shampoo. Shannon wished she could hold him tight and never let him go. Instead she smiled. "Are you hungry?"

The little boy nodded vigorously. "Want ice cream."

"That's my boy."

Shannon whirled to find Oliver standing in the doorway, his hair mussed from sleep, Barnaby at his feet.

She glanced at the clock on the wall. "You didn't sleep very long today."

It wasn't even six and he hadn't gotten to bed—or rather to sleep—until noon. Ollie had been taking an extra-long nap and they'd been...occupied.

Oliver's normal pattern was to sleep until seven, then they'd have a late supper. She usually fed Ollie earlier, as the child preferred to eat smaller, more frequent meals.

"Couldn't you sleep?" she asked, when he didn't respond.

"Too much on my mind" was all he said, but she could see his expression was troubled.

Shannon set a now-squirming Ollie to the floor. He immediately ran to his father.

Oliver scooped him up and a smile lifted his lips. "You getting some loving from Shannon? Smart man."

The child turned his head and smiled at Shannon. "Mama give ice cream."

Oliver raised a brow, but there was laughter in his eyes. "Now I see what goes on while I'm sleeping."

"Give ice cream, Mama," Ollie repeated, pointing in the direction of the refrigerator.

Neither she nor Oliver paid any attention to the boy calling her "Mama." After the night they'd played cards, Shannon had tried again to get Ollie to call her by her given name—even a shortened version—but she'd had to concede defeat.

"Ollie may want ice cream," Shannon said easily, casting a playful glance at the child, "but he'll be getting yogurt."

Oliver grimaced.

"Hey," she told him, "it's healthy and it tastes good."

"I'll take your word on that." He sniffed the air. "Whatever is in that pot smells good."

"Homemade vegetable beef soup," she told him. "My mom gave me her old bread machine, so I made tomato basil bread to go with the soup."

"Sounds delicious."

"I thought we'd start off with a glass of wine and antipasto. Then a green salad, soup and bread." Shannon, who'd practically kicked and screamed while her mother taught her to cook, had discovered she actually enjoyed cooking…when she had someone to cook for besides herself.

Oliver swung Ollie through the air, and the boy erupted into giggles. When he set him down, Ollie began to protest until Oliver flicked on the television to a *Daniel Tiger's Neighborhood* rerun.

Mesmerized, the boy crawled up onto the sofa and Barnaby jumped up with him. Shannon got him a tube of yogurt and the child took it, his eyes firmly focused on the television.

"What do you say?" Oliver said automatically.

"Tank you," came the response from the child.

Oliver moved to the table and pulled out a chair. "I got another email from Diane's mother."

Ah, so that's what has him so troubled.

Shannon went to the counter where she'd placed two wineglasses and poured each of them a glass. She set the plate of antipasto on the table and took a seat opposite Oliver.

As she munched on an olive and sipped her wine, she thought back to when he'd received the first email. It had been right after the card party. Though he'd mentioned it in passing, she could see he was troubled by the contact.

She hadn't pressed, knowing he would tell her the specifics in his own time, or he wouldn't. As then, she had to resist the urge to push.

"She wants to video chat with Ollie. Says he's their only grandchild and they want to be a part of his life." Anger, at odds with the calm delivery, simmered in the air.

Unsure how to respond, Shannon took a bite of ham.

Oliver set down his wineglass and leveled a gaze at her. "They expect me to go out of my way when they couldn't be bothered to tell me about Diane's death. I had to hear about her death at a bloody cocktail party."

"I assume you asked why they hadn't told you when you picked Ollie up." Shannon kept her tone nonchalant, as if totally unaware of the hostility vibrating in the air.

"Celeste—that's Diane's mother—said she hadn't been thinking clearly. That her daughter's death had devastated her."

"Sounds…logical."

As if he'd finally found an outlet for his rage, Oliver pinned his gaze on her. "You're on their side. You think I should forgive them."

"I think—" Shannon carefully picked up another olive, though her stomach was so jittery she didn't dare put it in her mouth "—that losing a child *would* be horrific. It seems logical she wasn't thinking clearly."

"They had Ollie for two months." He shoved back his chair and jerked to his feet. "Two months without notifying me."

Let it go, Shannon told herself, *you're the nanny. This isn't your business.*

But even as the thought crossed her mind, she realized that she couldn't let it go. She cared for Oliver and for his son.

Ollie deserved to know his grandparents. And no good would be served for Oliver to harbor such anger. Still, how to proceed was the question.

Shannon took a long drink of wine. "What was your impression of Diane's parents? Prior to her death, I mean?"

He turned back from the kitchen window where he'd been gazing—or rather *glaring*—out into the twilight.

"Nice enough," he said grudgingly, as if it pained him to say the words. "Father is a barrister. Mother is involved in a lot of civic activities."

"Any other children?" she asked casually.

"Just Diane."

"Did you see her parents often after you were married?"

"At holidays. Occasionally they'd come to London and we'd go to the symphony or the theater."

"No backyard barbecues or card parties?" Shannon teased, relieved when he smiled.

"Not their cup of tea." His smile faded. "I can see where you're headed with this, what you're trying to do."

"Really?" She lifted the glass to her lips, but didn't drink. "Tell me. What is it I'm trying to do?"

"You want me to think about what they were like before, to give them the benefit of the doubt." He twirled the stem of the glass between his fingers.

"Someday Ollie will want to know about his mother. He'll have all sorts of questions. Who better to give him that information than her parents?"

His jaw jutted out at a stubborn angle. "They should have told me."

"Life is full of should-haves," Shannon said with a heavy sigh. "I should have confronted Jerry, but I didn't. Cut them some slack, Oliver. Not only for Ollie's sake, but for your own."

Chapter Sixteen

Shannon rested her head against the seat of Oliver's luxury Mercedes sedan and let the soothing tones of a Mozart piano concerto wash over her. As the car continued smoothly down the highway toward town, she slanted a glance at Oliver. Her heart tripped when he returned her smile then reached over to squeeze her hand.

She liked that they didn't feel the need to talk all the time. They'd both gotten comfortable with occasional silence. And she liked how when she did say something, Oliver listened to her, really and truly listened. Though Shannon still didn't know what he planned to do about the situation with Oliver's grandparents, it had been empowering for her to realize that he seriously considered her opinions.

Tonight she planned to simply sit back and enjoy her date with Oliver.

It *was* a date, she told herself. How could it be considered anything else?

Oliver had asked if she was busy Saturday night.

She'd said she was free.

He asked if she wanted to check out the recently renovated theater that had opened in Horseback Hollow.

She told him she'd love to see a movie.

While Horseback Hollow wasn't big enough to support a first-run theater—they had to go to Vicker's Corners or Lubbock for that—this week the local theater was running the classic *Back to the Future*. Shannon hadn't even been born when the movie had been made, but since this particular science-fiction comedy was one of her father's favorites, she'd seen it many times.

The thought of sitting in a dark theater with Oliver, eating popcorn and candy, perhaps even sharing a soda, made seeing the movie for what had to be the zillionth time very appealing.

Josephine had been desperate for what she had taken to calling her "Ollie time," so the boy was spending the night with "Nana," whom he now adored. Thinking of the vibrant woman brought to mind something Shannon had meant to bring up earlier.

"Have you noticed that lately your mother is always texting?" she asked Oliver after he parked and they started down the sidewalk of Horseback Hollow's main street.

Earlier when they dropped off Ollie, Josephine had been in the process of sending a text. Though Shannon's parents both texted occasionally, lately it seemed every time she saw Oliver's mother, the phone was glued to her hand.

"Mum likes technology," he said a bit absently. His eyes suddenly widened and a grin split his face. "Brodie."

· Shannon hadn't seen much of Oliver's brother, although she knew he and Oliver had gotten together several times since Brodie had arrived in Horseback Hollow. From the few things Oliver had said, Shannon had the distinct impression his brother didn't think much of her hometown.

Brodie strode over. As always, he was impeccably dressed in a dark suit, his shoes shined to a high gloss. He cast a disapproving gaze at the jeans and cotton shirt Oliver wore.

"At least you're not wearing cowboy boots," Brodie said with a sniff.

"No," Shannon said with an impish smile, extending one foot so he could see her Tony Lama footwear. "I am."

A pained look crossed Brodie's face.

"We're going to view a movie at the cinema," Oliver told him. "Would you care to join us?"

"They're showing *Back to the Future*," Shannon added. "It's considered a classic."

A hint of a smile lifted Brodie's lips and then it was gone. It was as if he wasn't sure if she was putting him on or not. "I appreciate the invitation, but I have other plans."

"Would those plans involve Alden Moore?" Oliver lifted a brow. "I saw you coming out of the Hollows Cantina yesterday with him."

Shannon glanced at Oliver in surprise. He hadn't mentioned anything to her about his brother and Mr. Moore. Not that Oliver was required to tell her everyone he saw or spoke with during the course of the day. But Alden Moore was big news in Horseback Hollow.

The president of Moore Entertainment, Alden was the man charged with opening Cowboy Country USA, a theme park currently under construction at the edge of Horseback Hollow. The last Shannon heard, the park was scheduled to open Memorial Day weekend.

"The Hollows is one of the few places in town I can tolerate." Brodie gave a dismissive wave. "Thank heavens

I leave for London in a few days, where I can get some real food."

"What were you and Alden discussing?" Oliver pressed.

"Business. That's the only topic that interests me." Brodie shifted his gaze to Shannon, not missing the way his brother's hand circled her waist. "It appears you two are enjoying an evening out, leaving my nephew to fend for himself."

Oliver laughed. "Mum has him. Trust me, he'll be spoiled rotten by the time we pick him up tomorrow morning."

Surprise had Brodie's eyes widening. "You're leaving the tyke in her care overnight?"

"She insisted." Oliver's lips twitched. "You know how determined she can be."

"He'll be asleep by the time the movie is over," Shannon added. "We'd just have to wake him to take him home."

"Well—" Brodie inclined his head "—enjoy the cinema."

"Stop by before you leave," Oliver called after him.

Brodie nodded and continued to walk.

"Odd," Oliver said, almost to himself.

"What?"

"Brodie isn't usually so reticent." Oliver lifted a shoulder in a slight shrug. "It's of no importance."

He took Shannon's hand, a gesture that had come to seem so natural to him. Oliver assumed it was because there was a lot of touching going on at home.

Shannon's capacity for pleasure astounded him, as did his need for her. As their trust in each other had grown, they'd become even more adventurous in bed. Oliver had discovered that lovemaking could be passionate and intense but also casual and fun. Last night he'd even laughed aloud while tussling with her on the bed.

As they strolled down the sidewalk, under the glow of the streetlamps, they spoke of Ollie and Barnaby, of his mother and other family members. She didn't mention Diane's parents and he didn't bring them up either. Though he was becoming more reconciled to the idea of letting them be a part of Ollie's life, he wasn't quite there yet.

Once they reached the box office, he paid for the tickets. Shannon tried to pay for hers but that was never an option. He had invited her and he would pay.

Though the show was ready to begin, Shannon insisted she couldn't watch the movie without candy and popcorn. He hurriedly bought the refreshments and they found a couple of seats toward the back of the darkened theater. The place was only a third full, so there were plenty of choices.

"I love Junior Mints," Shannon whispered halfway through the show, popping another of the dark candies into her mouth.

The merest hint of chocolate remained on her lips. Leaning close, he ran a finger across her lips, heard her quick intake of air.

"Chocolate," he said, in response to her questioning look. "Your lips are sweet enough. They don't need any enhancement."

Instead of looking at the screen, where a truck of manure was being dumped on Biff's car, Shannon's gaze remained focused on Oliver. His groin tightened when she slowly ran her tongue across her lips.

Oliver had never condoned public displays of affection. But lately he found himself reaching for Shannon's hand or placing his palm against her back...simply for the contact and because the connection to her felt so good.

Taking her arm to steady her when getting out of the

car made perfect sense. Reaching out to grab her if she stumbled was totally appropriate.

Kissing a woman in a public theater? Unthinkable. But now, as Oliver's gaze lingered on Shannon's full, soft lips, he found he couldn't think of anything else.

Wait until you get home.

He'd never last that long.

Wait until you get in the car.

He'd never last that long.

Kiss her now. It seemed the best option. The *only* option. Societal rules be damned.

"Shannon," he spoke softly while his gaze traveled over her face and searched her eyes.

Was that harsh, uneven breath coming from her? Or him?

With great tenderness, Oliver brushed his fingers against her cheek then slowly lowered his head and closed his mouth over hers.

The kiss was warm and sweet and touched a place inside him that had been cold for so long. He heard sounds of laughter coming from the big screen but paid it no mind. All that mattered was him. And her. The closeness. The love.

The thought had him jerking back.

Even in the dim light, he could see the startled confusion in her eyes. Her lipstick was smudged from his kisses, the hair she'd intricately braided pulling loose.

Though his heart galloped in his chest, he casually gestured with his head toward the screen. "They're getting to the good part."

Since he'd paid little attention to the film, he had no idea what had happened or was about to happen. Neither did he particularly care.

Shannon gave a jerky nod and turned her attention back to the screen, but he sensed her puzzlement. When she straightened in her seat and leaned ever so slightly away from him, her withdrawal was like an ice pick to the heart.

Oliver slid his arm around her and pulled her close. When she relaxed and rested her head against his shoulder, his world that had tipped so precariously only seconds before righted itself.

He knew they were back to normal when she lifted the box of Junior Mints from her lap and offered him one.

Though Oliver wasn't a fan of the candies, he took one and realized when it hit his tongue that it tasted like her kisses. And he simply had to have another taste. The rest of the movie passed by unwatched.

Shannon blinked as they stepped from the darkened theater into the light. She looked, he thought fancifully, like a sleeping beauty waking up. *His* sleeping beauty.

Her lips were swollen from his kisses, her hair mussed. He hadn't been able to keep from slipping his fingers into the silky strands as their mouths melded together. And though they'd just stopped kissing when the credits had begun to roll, Oliver was seized with an overpowering urge to kiss her again.

Actually, he wanted to do a whole lot more than kiss her.

"Instead of going for ice cream in Vicker's Corners as we discussed, how about we go home and have…dessert there?" Though Shannon spoke casually, he recognized the look in her eye.

"Great minds think alike." He took her arm as they stepped out of the theater and onto the sidewalk.

Oliver resisted—barely—the urge to hurry her along. There was no need to rush. With his mum watching Ollie, they had all night.

"Oliver, what a pleasant surprise."

He pulled up short. "Amelia."

Looking young and carefree in a dress more suited to a college girl than a new mum, his sister quickly closed the distance between them. Quinn was with her, their baby bound to his chest in some kind of flowery fabric.

Oliver shot him a sympathetic glance.

Quinn simply grinned.

"What are you two doing out?" Oliver asked. The baby seemed far too small to be exposed to the cool night air.

"We could ask you the same question." Amelia's decidedly curious gaze slid from him to Shannon.

"We wanted to check out the new theater," Shannon said, then seemed to reconsider her words. "I mean, I wanted to check it out so I asked Oliver if he'd be interested in joining me. He said he was, so here we are."

She was chattering, Oliver realized, the way she tended to do when she was nervous. Why, he wondered, was she so nervous? And why was she making it sound as if he'd simply tagged along for the evening?

"It was very nice, wasn't it, Oliver?" she added, when no one spoke.

"It was very enjoyable." The only part Oliver remembered of the movie was the rolling credits, but the kisses had been exceedingly pleasurable. "What about you?"

"Wendy and Marcos wanted to see Clementine, so we stopped in for dessert."

Oliver resisted—barely—slanting a glance at Shannon. They had a different kind of dessert planned once they reached home. And he had no doubt he'd enjoy his more than whatever his sister and her husband ordered tonight.

"Where's Ollie?" Amelia glanced around as if expecting the toddler to jump out from behind a tree.

"He's with Mum this evening."

"Ollie is such a sweet little boy." Amelia's lips curved, her look one of fondness. "I was telling Quinn just the other day how much I wished you and Ollie would stay in Horseback Hollow."

"Am, you know that's—" Oliver began.

"Oliver was such a good big brother to me," Amelia told Shannon. "I couldn't have asked for better. I know our children are just cousins, but if Ollie grew up here, he'd be like Clemmie's big brother."

Amelia shifted her gaze back to Oliver. "Wouldn't that be nice?"

"Most certainly." Oliver knew his sister too well to argue. "But my home is in London."

"It doesn't have to be," Amelia said, her expression earnest. "Technology makes it possible for people to work from anywhere. Quinn and I watched an episode on the telly about that quite recently."

"Did you?" Oliver said, vaguely amused at the thought of his former jet-setting younger sister sitting at home watching the telly and discussing changing work habits with her rancher husband.

"You're conducting your business right now from Horseback Hollow," Amelia reminded him, as if she somehow thought that fact had slipped his mind.

"He is, but it's very difficult for him." Shannon spoke up for the first time since Amelia had started her discourse. "Because of the time difference, Oliver has to do all his work in the middle of the night."

"Granted, it's probably not ideal," Amelia conceded. "But if you wanted, you could make staying here work."

Once again, Oliver avoided arguing and simply agreed with his headstrong baby sister. "You're right, Amelia. If a person wants something badly enough, they can make it happen."

* * *

Though it was past midnight and Oliver had a lot of calls to make, he sat back in his desk chair, his mind on everything but stocks and bonds.

The words he'd said to Amelia—primarily to placate her—continued to haunt him. Three days might have passed, but he couldn't stop thinking about them.

He believed what he'd said. If he wanted something badly enough, he could make it happen. In his case, Oliver wanted Shannon.

Though he hadn't yet said the words, he realized somewhere along the way, he'd fallen in love with her. Here was a woman he could trust, a woman who cared for him as much as he did for her.

He'd learned a lot from his failed relationship with Diane. Oliver accepted part of the blame for the demise of his first marriage. Back then he'd showed his love the only way he knew how—by providing the material things she so desperately craved.

They'd had the house in the country, the one in London. He'd given her expensive jewelry and household help to make her life easier. But he realized now those were only things. He'd held back his heart. Or perhaps it was simply that his heart had been waiting for someone else.

Though he'd never say that aloud—it was much too Lord Byron-ish—he believed it. While it was still difficult for him to verbalize emotions, Shannon had taught him that actions had to be coupled with words.

That's what Oliver planned to do tonight. His fingers closed around the small jeweler's box in his pocket. When he'd been in Lubbock yesterday, he'd seen the perfect ring for Shannon in a small jewelry store's window.

A large marquis-cut diamond solitaire, comparable to

anything the Harry Winston jewelry company would carry, had caught his eye.

Oliver had never been a foolish man, or an impulsive one. He and Diane had dated for several years and he'd spent a lot of time considering whether he should propose. Only now did he realize that if he had to put so much thought into it—at one point he'd even drafted a list of the pros and cons—she hadn't been the one for him.

He'd settled, plain and simple. He'd been past thirty, he wanted a home and a family, and on paper they appeared well suited. But not once had Diane made his heart beat faster simply by walking into a room. Even worse, their house had never felt like a home.

With Shannon, Oliver could fully relax and be himself. No pretense, no posturing. She loved and accepted him as he was and, because he had her unqualified support, he wanted to be a better man.

She's never said she loves you.

The doubt surfaced and though he tried to brush it away, it kept returning to buzz around in his head, like a troublesome fly.

Oliver recognized this hesitation—knew the fear arose from those early years when his father had slapped down any talk or show of emotion.

It was no wonder his mother had left the man. Soon enough for Brodie not to have been tainted by his father's cold harshness, but not soon enough for Oliver.

But he'd gotten past that, Oliver told himself. Telling Ollie he loved him now came easier. And, once he said the words to Shannon, he vowed never to stop saying them.

In his mind, the only thing standing between them now was her affection for Horseback Hollow. But he felt confident of his ability to convince her she could find happiness in London with him and Ollie.

Tomorrow, he would confess his love. They would marry and meld their lives together.

For now, he had a business to run.

Oliver picked up his mobile phone and got back to work.

Chapter Seventeen

"I'm so happy you stopped by this afternoon." Shannon opened the oven door, releasing the delicious aroma of cinnamon into the kitchen. "Otherwise I'd have to eat this coffee cake all by myself."

"You've got Oliver," Rachel reminded her, sipping her coffee. "What time will he be up?"

Shannon lifted the pan to a cooling rack, then took off the oven mitts and tossed them to the counter. She glanced at the clock, saw it was just past four. "He didn't go to bed until almost two, so I don't expect him up until seven. Perhaps even later."

She saw no reason to mention Ollie had been taking a nap when his father had concluded his business dealings at noon. She and Oliver had taken advantage of the opportunity. Though Oliver had been in bed—with her—there had been no sleeping involved.

Rachel studied Shannon over the rim of her cup. "I thought you were supposed to get off at five."

Shannon dropped into the chair opposite Rachel. "Oliver would never get any sleep if I left so early."

Her friend clucked her tongue, reminding Shannon of her mother. "Some things never change."

The coffee cup Shannon had been raising to her lips returned to the table with a clatter. "What's that supposed to mean?"

"It means you let people run all over you."

For a second, Shannon was stunned. She wasn't sure how to respond. Could she have misheard? Transposed some of her mother's words into Rachel's mouth? "What did you say?"

"I meant no disrespect. I care about you." Rachel reached across the table and took Shannon's hands. Before speaking, she slanted a sideways glance where Ollie sat playing with his blocks, Barnaby supervising. "Think about it. Jerry comes on to you. Sure, you tell him you want none of it. But not forcefully enough to make him understand you mean business. He persists. Instead of filing charges or even threatening to, you ran away."

Heat flooded Shannon's face and she pulled her hands back. She rose and moved to the counter. Though the coffee cake was still too warm, she cut it anyway. It gave her something to do with her hands while her thoughts tumbled like clothes in an out-of-control dryer at the local Laundromat.

Though what had occurred at her previous job had happened pretty much the way Rachel described it, she *had* tried to speak with Jerry.

"I was forceful," Shannon protested. "I told him so many different ways to bug off, it wasn't even funny. But he didn't hear me. He didn't want to hear what I had to say, because I didn't matter."

"Now you're doing the same thing with Oliver." Rachel

leaned forward, resting her forearms on the table. "You set up parameters—like you're off at five every day—but then you don't hold him to them. He walks all over you, and worse yet, you don't seem to notice or care."

Ollie let out a shriek when his blocks came crashing down.

"Ollie, shush, your daddy is sleeping," Shannon said automatically, then refocused on Rachel. "What you said about Oliver, it's not like that between us."

"Of course it is. You just don't want to see it."

"You're wrong." A tightness filled Shannon's chest, making it difficult to breathe. "I want to help him out. I like taking care of Ollie."

Rachel's gaze searched her face. "You're in love with the Brit."

Shannon started to deny it, then decided why bother. Rachel knew her too well and would simply see right through her denial. She sighed. "I am."

Rachel inclined her head, her gaze speculative. "Does he love you, too?"

Ah, that was the question.

She thought about what Amelia had said, that if you wanted to make something work, you'd do it. She'd give up her life in Horseback Hollow for Oliver...all he had to do was ask.

But what is he willing to give up for you? To do for you?

Shannon frowned. Maybe she was a pushover. She shoved the troubling thought aside.

"C'mon, Shannon," Rachel pressed. "Be honest, with me and with yourself."

"It feels as if he cares," Shannon said slowly. "When he looks at me, there's this warmth in his eyes. When he touches me, there's heat but something more, something deeper."

"Heat. Warmth. You did it, babe." There was admiration in Rachel's voice. "When we made that bet, I thought for sure I'd win, but sounds like you heated up the iceberg. I owe you a drink."

Oliver paused in the hallway. He'd been jolted awake by the sound of Ollie crying out. But by the time his brain had cleared and he'd reached the living room, his son was happily playing with his bricks.

He'd intended to go back to bed until he heard Rachel's words. She and Shannon had a bet. A bet that involved him.

He clenched his stomach. How had he missed the signs? It wasn't as if this was a first. He'd been targeted before by women who wanted him for his stock portfolio and social position.

But Shannon hadn't been after his money. She'd done it simply for sport. Just to see if she could. And to his shame, she'd succeeded.

His father had been right, after all. A man who trusts was a fool.

Well, he wouldn't make that mistake again.

Though he returned to his bedroom, Oliver didn't sleep. Instead of the quiet candlelit dinner followed by a proposal tonight, once Rachel left, he would send Shannon on her way.

No one made a fool out of Oliver Fortune Hayes.

Not even the woman he'd been foolish enough to love.

Rachel left shortly after five and Shannon had just fed Ollie when Oliver walked into the kitchen.

"Hey, I thought you wouldn't be up for another two hours." She crossed the room to him, lifting her face for the expected kiss.

Instead, he brushed past her. Opening the kitchen cupboard, he took out the bottle of whiskey and poured himself a shot. He drank the amber liquid as if it was water and he was dying of thirst.

"Is something wrong?" she asked tentatively.

"Has Ollie been fed?"

"Just finished. He ate like a little piggy, so he's probably going to need changing soon." She shut her mouth before she could ramble even more.

Oliver was clearly upset over something, and all she could talk about was his son's diapers?

"What's wrong?" she asked quietly.

Though she longed to wrap her arms around him and hold him close, she stayed where she stood. It was as if he had this invisible force field around him warning of danger should one get too close.

"It's not working." He poured another shot, downed the contents of the glass again in a single gulp.

A cold chill slithered down her spine. "What isn't?"

"This." He gestured wildly, the empty glass in his hands. "You. Me. You taking care of Ollie."

"Wait a minute." Breathe, she told herself. Stay calm and breathe. "Things are good between us. Ollie is happy and I thought—" her voice trailed off slightly before she reined it back in "—things were good between you and me, too."

He turned and met her gaze, his eyes looking more gray than blue, and cold as steel. "I know about the bet."

"Bet?" She pulled her brows together. "What bet?"

"The one you made with Rachel." His fingers tightened around the glass until his knuckles turned white. "How you were going to thaw the iceberg, as you ladies put it. Well, congratulations. You may have won the bet but you lost the job. You're fired."

Shannon stared at him, trying to process what he was

saying. "That thing between Rachel and me was just a joke. When you first came into town, Rachel said—"

"I'm not interested in your excuses." His voice sliced like a knife through the air.

"I want you out of here in—" he glanced at his watch "—ten minutes."

For a second, Shannon thought she might faint. Or burst into tears. Instead she simply stood there, her body frozen in place.

This was all a simple misunderstanding, she wanted to say. But what would be the point? She'd tried to explain but he wouldn't listen.

Oliver didn't want to hear what she had to say. Because she didn't matter.

That was the one thing she hadn't been able to make Rachel understand.

That when you don't matter to someone, you might as well talk to the wind.

Fully aware that her unexpected appearance at the Triple S ranch would bring a ton of questions she preferred not to answer, instead of going home Shannon drove to Vicker's Corners. She rented a room at a quaint old Victorian B and B that had caught her eye when she and Rachel were shopping.

Last week, she'd hoped that before Oliver left town, they could carve out some time and spend the night here.

Well, she was here. But she was alone.

Shannon put her suitcase on the floor and flopped back on the bed, still dry-eyed. The tears were there, all balled up inside her. For now she was keeping them under tight control, afraid if she started crying, she might never stop.

Coming to a parting of ways was for the best, she told herself. Oliver would soon be returning to London anyway. By then she'd likely have her new job with the Fortune Foundation.

She tried to tell herself she'd been prepared for the fact that Oliver and Ollie would eventually leave, but she knew that was a lie. The truth was, she'd been secretly hoping Oliver would stay or ask her to go with him and Ollie to London.

Boy, had she been off the mark. He hadn't even cared enough to listen to her. No way was that love. Not the kind of love she wanted, anyway.

It was for the best, she told herself for the zillionth time.

When a stray tear slipped down her cheek, she hurriedly brushed it aside. She always felt like crying when she was tired. Perhaps, if she closed her eyes for just a second…

Shannon woke to sunlight streaming through the lace curtains. Groggy, she turned and saw that it was morning. The vintage alarm clock on the nightstand read 8:00 a.m.

The proprietress, a perky woman named Bea, had gone into great detail when Shannon had checked in about the lovely breakfast served daily between six and ten.

The last thing Shannon wanted to do was make small talk with strangers. She felt hollow and empty inside. But she refused to sit in the room all day and mope. She would visit her favorite Vicker's Corners café, the one that served the best granola pancakes in the entire state.

Even if the mere thought of eating made her stomach churn, she could sit outside in the sunshine and enjoy the fresh air. She would order a cup of their special coffee—a dark roast and chicory blend with steamed milk.

Feeling better now that she had a plan, Shannon headed for the shower. Minutes later, feeling decidedly more human, she pulled her hair back from her face with a couple of clips, grabbed a pair of jeans and a cotton shirt in heartbreak red—totally appropriate for today—and left the B and B via the back door.

The air held a crisp edge and walking briskly calmed her. It took her less than five minutes to reach the café. Though the café's outdoor seating was surprisingly full for a weekday, Shannon snagged a small wrought-iron table for two. She ordered pancakes—just in case her appetite came back—and coffee. She was scrolling through Facebook pages when her phone rang.

For a second her heart leaped. But it wasn't Oliver's name on the readout—not that she wanted to speak with him anyway—it was Rachel's. Better, she decided, and although they weren't on a FaceTime video call, she smiled. She'd read somewhere that even if you didn't mean it, a smile could be heard in your voice. "Good morning, Rach."

"Are you busy?"

"Not at all." Shannon smiled her thanks to the waiter who placed a steaming cup of coffee in front of her. "What's up?"

A long moment of silence filled the air.

"You haven't heard."

Shannon's heart seized. She set down the coffee cup with carefully controlled movements. "Heard what?"

Another few heartbeats. "I thought for sure they'd have called you."

Was it her parents? Oliver? Or, oh dear God no...Ollie? Her heart stopped, then began to gallop. The toddler was so quick, she didn't even know if Oliver realized how fast. If you didn't watch him every second, he could easily be hurt.

"Who?" Shannon's voice rose despite her best efforts to control it. "Tell me."

"Christopher Fortune."

Shannon's breath came out in a whoosh and she slumped back in her seat, relief leaving her weak. "Thank God."

"What did you say?"

"I said, that's great." But the moment the words left her lips, Shannon wondered why Christopher Fortune would be calling Rachel. She didn't have to wait long for the answer.

"I got the job." Rachel spoke quickly, as if she wanted to get it all out before she was interrupted. "In fact I'm at the Foundation office now. They have a bunch of employment forms for me to fill out."

"That's…wonderful. Fabulous news." Shannon did her best to force some enthusiasm into her voice, even as the realization hit. They'd hired Rachel, a woman with no marketing experience, instead of her. "I'm—I'm happy for you. Congratulations."

"You're probably wondering why they hired me and not you." Rachel's voice held a nervous edge.

Shannon paused. "Uh, maybe just a little."

The waiter delivered her pancakes and Shannon offered him a brief smile of thanks as her mind raced.

This didn't make sense. Sure, Rachel was pretty and smart, but so was she. And Shannon had three years of experience in the field. Christopher had been impressed by that fact, Shannon recalled.

"Well, I found out something that I think you need to know."

"I don't know, Rachel." Shannon expelled a heavy sigh. Did she really want to know that Christopher thought she'd blown the interview? Because what other reason could there be for her not getting the position? "What's done is done."

Rachel gave a disgusted snort. "How are you ever going to stand up for yourself when you insist on keeping your head in a hole?"

Shannon dumped some syrup on the pancakes. "Okay, tell me."

"The temp who's been working here is real chatty. She told me I almost didn't get the job because I didn't have the experience."

The piece of pancake that had been halfway to Shannon's mouth froze in midair. Her heart began to thud.

"She told me the other person they were considering got a bad reference from her previous employer," Rachel continued. "Apparently that swayed the decision in my direction."

"May I join you?"

Shannon looked up, startled, when a man's hand closed over the empty seat at her table.

Brodie Fortune Hayes may have asked Shannon the question, but he'd decided to join her regardless of the answer.

This morning, when Brodie had called his brother and asked Oliver if he wanted to check out how the Cowboy Country theme park was coming along, Oliver had nearly bitten his head off.

Something was clearly troubling his older sibling. When Brodie saw Nanny Shannon sitting alone, so far from home and without her little charge, he decided to do some investigating. While Brodie hadn't been able to get anything out of his closemouthed brother, he believed he'd have better luck with the woman.

Shannon covered the phone with her hand. "Sorry. Not in the mood for company this morning."

Ignoring her, he sat and motioned to the waiter for some coffee.

She shot him a venomous glance. He responded with a bland smile, pulling out his phone to check the stock reports. Oliver wasn't the only Fortune Hayes with a healthy portfolio.

"Jerry torpedoed me," Shannon muttered into the phone.

Brodie kept his gaze focused on his mobile unit, sensing she'd watch her words more carefully if she knew he was listening.

"It had to be that, Rachel. He's the reason I didn't get the job." Shannon breathed in and out, and Brodie watched in fascination as she fought for control. "If he thinks I'm going to let him get away with doing this to me, he's got a surprise coming. I—"

Shannon turned her back to Brodie and listened for several seconds.

"I don't think he'd physically harm me. I'll be fine, Rach. You told me to stop being a doormat…okay, maybe you didn't use those exact words, but that's what you meant. I'm just telling you. He's not getting away with this. Okay, bye."

Shannon set the phone down on the table and fixed her gaze on Brodie.

"Are you worried someone might do you physical harm?" Brodie demanded. "Is Oliver aware you might be in danger?"

"I'm not in danger." Her tone was as flat as her eyes. "Even if I were, I can take care of myself."

"Does Oliver know?"

"There's nothing to know. Besides, your brother and I aren't exactly on speaking terms at the moment."

"Oh?" Brodie lifted a brow and feigned surprise. "What happened?"

She hesitated for so long he wondered if he needed to ask again. But just as he opened his mouth to press a little more, she began to speak.

"You want to know? Well, I'll tell you. Oliver used some

ridiculous teasing bet I made with Rachel as an excuse to get rid of me. He couldn't even listen to my explanation. You know why?" Obviously the question was rhetorical because she plowed ahead, not waiting for his response. "Because I don't matter to him. He knows me. He knows my heart. But he doesn't care and he just wanted me gone."

Shannon jerked to her feet. "Thanks for breakfast, Brodie." She gestured to the waiter, who'd arrived to take the man's order. "He'll take my check, too."

Without a backward glance, she strode off.

Strange, Brodie thought, *yet very interesting.* He pulled out his phone to call his brother.

Chapter Eighteen

He had behaved abysmally.

For a man who prided himself on his integrity, it was hard for Oliver to admit that what his father had done—what he'd given the man the power to do—had caused him to overreact and treat the woman he loved in such a despicable manner. Shannon had seen through him. Her accusations had been spot-on.

He'd used the "bet" as an excuse to push her away, even though he knew in his heart she wasn't capable of such duplicity. It had been the move of a coward.

What he and Shannon shared didn't have anything to do with a wager. Even if their physical relationship had started that way—which he didn't believe it had—what was between the two of them, the closeness they shared, was one hundred percent genuine.

Oliver now faced the task of righting a very large wrong. But he firmly believed the words he'd said to his sister;

that if a man wanted something badly enough, he could make it happen. He would win Shannon back. He would show her he could be the man she deserved.

He was on his way to the Triple S when Brodie called and relayed the puzzling conversation he'd overheard. Oliver pulled over to the side of the road. His mind raced as he put the pieces together.

"Daddy, cookie," Ollie called from his car seat.

"In a second, son," Oliver said, despite knowing he hadn't packed any biscuits. Even as he ordered Amelia's number to be dialed, he decided the tiger Diane's parents had given Ollie would have to do in place of a biscuit. He leaned over the seat and tossed the well-loved soft toy to him.

The boy squealed with delight and hugged the tiger to his chest.

Oliver stared thoughtfully at his son, at the toy given in love, then shifted his focus as the ringing stopped and Amelia answered. As he'd hoped, she had Rachel's mobile number. Another call confirmed his greatest fear. According to her friend, Shannon was already on her way to Lubbock to confront her former boss. And she'd gone alone.

Oliver dropped off Ollie at his sister's house, then attempted to ring Shannon again. She didn't pick up. He hadn't really expected her to and was once again on the highway headed to Lubbock.

His hands clenched the steering wheel in a death grip. If that sod touched one hair on Shannon's head, Oliver Fortune Hayes would make him sorry he was ever born.

The rental vehicle's GPS led him directly to a large office building of steel and glass in the downtown business district. The lack of parking in the area was of no concern to a Fortune. Oliver simply pulled the Mercedes sedan into a loading zone in front of the building and hopped out.

He barreled through the front door…and straight into Shannon.

He wrapped his arms around her, holding her so tight, she squeaked.

"Oliver, let go, you're crushing me."

Loosening his hold, he stepped back, studying her from head to toe. "Are you okay? Did he hurt you?"

"Who?"

"Your former boss. The one you came to see."

"I told him what I was going to do and I did it." For a moment, a smile of smug satisfaction lifted her lips. "I went to human resources and filed a sexual harassment complaint against him. Apparently the company takes such charges very seriously."

For a moment, it was as if yesterday had never happened. The connection, the warmth was still there. Had yesterday been a bad dream? Perhaps they would simply move forward, relegating his bad behavior to the past.

"You're a strong and brave woman." Oliver gave a little laugh. "Although, you may have taken several years off my life during the drive here."

For a second she returned his smile, then seemed to remember how things were between them. She took several very deliberate steps back.

It appeared forgiveness wasn't going to come so easily.

When Shannon turned abruptly on her heel and started walking, he followed.

She whirled and narrowed her gaze. "What is it you want, Oliver? Why are you even here?"

The coolness in her gaze sent a chill down his spine.

"I should think it'd be fairly obvious." He moved to adjust his cuffs, then realized he'd left the house in such a hurry he'd grabbed the nearest item of clothing. He looked down and saw he'd pulled on an old gray sweatshirt that Shannon had borrowed from her father the other night.

Though he tried to ignore the fact he was dressed like a country bumpkin, his confidence was shaken. "My brother called. I spoke with Rachel. I feared for your well-being."

She offered a tight smile, one that didn't come close to reaching her eyes. "As you can see for yourself, I'm quite fine."

"Well, I'm not quite fine. I haven't been since you left."

"You mean since you ordered me from your home? Since you fired me without even listening to me? When you didn't even give me a chance to say a proper goodbye to Ollie?"

That *had* been a mistake. His son had been distraught. All Oliver could think of to placate the boy was to tell him Shannon's mum needed her for a few days.

Oliver raked his hand through his hair. "We need to talk."

She opened her mouth, then shut it and considered. "There's a park just around the corner. I guess there are a few things I need to say to you."

Her tone wasn't promising, but he consoled himself that at least she was willing to hear him out. But when they reached the small green oasis and took a seat on an ornate metal bench beside an evergreen that had been cut to resemble a dragon, she lifted a hand when he started to speak.

"You had your say yesterday. It's my turn." Shannon lifted her chin, her brown eyes flat and cool. "You were completely out of line. You overheard only part of a conversation, yet you ran with it. I've spent a considerable amount of time thinking why a logical man such as yourself would do something so illogical."

She jerked to her feet and began to pace. "I concluded

you were scared of what had been building between us. You were looking for a way to run. That bit of conversation you overheard gave you the out you were seeking."

Oliver opened his mouth to respond but shut it when she glared and continued. "That may have made you feel all justified and righteous, but it was devastating to me. To have the man I loved think so little of me. Worse, I just took the abuse and slunk away. Well, no more. Shannon Singleton is no one's doormat. Not anymore. Not ever again."

Though her voice was steady, she was visibly trembling.

He stood and would have stepped closer, but once again she held up a hand. The coolness in her eyes was like a knife to the heart. And the worst of it was, he had only himself to blame for the distance between them.

Oliver cleared his throat. "First I want to say, I'm proud of you, Shannon."

"Well, doesn't that make me feel all warm and fuzzy inside."

The sarcasm had him raising his brows. "I mean it. I know what it took for you to come down here. You're right about my behavior. I was out of line last night. Please come home with me. And Ollie. It's where you belong."

"News bulletin. I don't belong anyplace where someone can order me out of the house when they get angry or scared or whatever." Shannon leaned over and picked up her bag, which she'd set by the bench, then straightened. "That's not a home, that's a job."

"Shannon," he called out when she headed to the ornate entrance gate.

After a slight hesitation, she stopped and turned.

"I'm sorry," he said.

She paused for the briefest of seconds, as if waiting for him to say more. After a long moment she gave a little laugh that somehow managed to sound incredibly sad. "Yeah, well, I'm sorry, too."

Before Oliver climbed the porch steps of the Singleton house, he cleaned off the bottom of his shoes. Who knew a walk through a corral could be so...unsavory?

Though it wasn't even ten in the morning, he'd already managed to cross two items off his agenda, as evidenced by the conciliatory email winging its way across the Atlantic to Diane's parents and his visit to the corral to speak with Shep.

His future father-in-law had been shocked when Oliver had shown up to ask for Shannon's hand in marriage. Actually, he thought, the man seemed vastly amused that Oliver wanted to marry a woman who wasn't even speaking to him at the present time.

Still, Shep had laughed and clapped him on the shoulder, telling him to "go for it." Oliver took that to mean he had the man's blessing.

Now came the hard part. After taking several deep breaths, he rang the bell.

Through the screen door, he watched Lilian approach. This time there was no broad welcoming smile, only a slightly wary one. Oliver didn't blame her. Shannon was her daughter and he was, well, the cad who'd hurt her.

"Hello, Oliver." Lilian glanced nervously over her shoulder. "I didn't expect to see you here."

"Mrs. Singleton," he said, reverting back to the more formal address. "I was wondering if you could fetch Shannon for me. I'd like to speak with her."

"Who is it, Mom?"

A second after he heard her voice, Shannon stood beside her mother and close enough to touch.

Oliver's heart slammed against his chest. She was

breathtakingly beautiful in blue jeans, a simple white shirt and bare feet.

Her eyes widened. "What are you doing here?"

Oliver met her confused gaze with a slightly unsteady one of his own. "I'm here to listen."

Shannon blinked. Her initial instinct had been to order him off the property. Until he said he'd come to *listen*. After she'd left the park, she'd thought of several other things she wanted to say to him.

In fact, she'd planned to call him today. She considered. For what she had to say, face-to-face would definitely be better.

"Okay, we'll talk." Shannon glanced at her mother. "Give us a few minutes."

Her mother's eyes softened. "Take as long as you need, dear."

Shannon stepped out onto the porch and, after a momentary hesitation, moved to the swing.

Oliver followed, taking a seat on the far end then swiveling to face her.

She had to admit he looked quite dashing in his dark suit, crisp white shirt and red Hermes tie. Once, when she told him wearing her favorite cowboy boots made her feel more confident, he'd sheepishly confessed he felt that same way about a suit and tie.

Her heart softened slightly. "You said you came here to listen."

He nodded.

"Well, then, I'd like to see Ollie." Shannon folded her hands in her lap, hoping he didn't notice the slight tremor. "I think it's important he understands I didn't leave because of anything he'd done."

"You can see him anytime you want," Oliver said. "Ollie has missed you. We both miss you."

The last was said so quietly, but with such emotion, that for a second Shannon found it difficult to speak. She took a moment to clear her throat. "I—I left a few things behind, too. Let me know when would be a good time to stop by."

"You're welcome anytime."

Tears stung the backs of her lids, but Shannon blinked rapidly and kept them at bay. "Okay, fine. Thanks."

He reached out as if he intended to take her hand but let it fall when she sat back.

"Is there anything else you want to say to me?" he asked.

Shannon thought for a moment, a task that was becoming increasingly difficult. His nearness appeared to have turned her brain to mush. Of course, five minutes after he left she'd likely recall a dozen things she wanted to say. "No. No. That was all."

"In that case, would you mind listening to me for a second?" When she opened her mouth, he lifted a hand. "If at any time you want me to leave or to stop talking, just say the word."

"Are you saying if I ask you to leave and never come back, you'll do it?" Though her insides shook like jelly, her voice came out steady.

"I can't promise I'll never come back." Oliver shifted in his seat. "You're too important to me to make such a promise."

"What do you want to say, Oliver?"

"You were absolutely right."

"About?"

"Deep down, I was fearful of allowing you to see how much you mattered to me. My father told me numerous times anyone who loves or shows emotion is a fool."

"You were married, Oliver. You'd taken that leap once before." Shannon's chuckle held no humor. "I'd have thought love would come easier to you the second time around."

"I was never able to give my heart totally to Diane." A red flush rose up his neck. "Since coming to Texas, I've come to believe my heart was waiting for you."

Shannon gaped. Never had she thought she'd hear such flowery prose come from Oliver's mouth. Yet he seemed sincere...if slightly embarrassed.

"I'm not proud of my behavior." His eyes closed for a second and she watched as he clenched and unclenched one hand. "When you walked out the door and drove off, I realized I'd been a berk."

"A what?"

"A—a fool." He gave her a lopsided smile. "You have my heart, you know. You will always have it." He reached over and took her hands in his. "Believe me. I love you. I trust you. Completely. Totally. Without reservation."

Tears welled in her eyes and slipped down her cheeks.

Oliver wiped them away with the pads of his fingers. "I'm sorry I hurt you."

"I love you, too." The emotion squeezing her heart made her voice husky.

"You realize Ollie and I are a package deal."

"I love Ollie." This time it was *her* fingers swiping at the tears that seemed determined to fall. "Your little guy stole my heart within seconds of meeting him."

"If we were to be together permanently, what is it you'd want, Shannon? Tell me what it is and it's yours."

Puzzled, she pulled her brows together. "What do you mean?"

"If we were married, where would you like to live?"

Married? Her breath caught. If they were *married*?

Shannon thought of how she'd insisted to Rachel she wouldn't wed any man unless he agreed to settle in Horseback Hollow. "What if I said I wanted to live in Horseback Hollow?"

"Then that's where we'll live," he said without hesitation. "I want you to be happy. If being here makes you happy, this is where we'll live."

"But your business," she protested. "The hours—"

Capturing her hand, he brought her fingers to his lips and kissed them one by one. "Don't worry. It won't be a problem."

He might be able to make it work, but she knew it'd be difficult not only for him, but for them as a family. Still, it appeared he was willing to make the sacrifice.

Because he loves me. Because he wants me to be happy.

Shannon loved her friends, her family and her little town. But there was a whole, wonderful—slightly scary—world out there she'd yet to explore. Was it fear that had made her so adamant about remaining in Horseback Hollow?

"Would we build a home in town? Or would you prefer living on a ranch? If you could pick," Oliver prompted, "tell me what your dream home would look like."

His blue eyes were focused on her. She had his full attention.

"In my perfect world—" she slid closer to him "—you'd have your arm around my shoulders during this discussion."

Before she'd finished speaking, Oliver closed the remaining distance between them and slipped an arm around her shoulders, pressing a kiss against her hair. "Better?"

"Much." The heat from his body mingled with hers and the coldness inside her began to thaw. "Actually, I'd like two homes."

He smiled. "That could be arranged. One in town, the other in the countryside, I presume?"

"Actually, I was thinking of one home here, the other in London. We could spend part of the year in England and the other part in Horseback Hollow. When Ollie is school-age, we might need to reconsider, but for now, that's what I'd like."

His brows pulled together. "Are you certain?"

"Yes." She kissed him on the lips. "Absolutely certain."

"Then that's what we'll do."

"Just like that?"

"Just like that." He smiled. "What about children?"

"What about them?"

"How many would you like?"

She hesitated.

"Be honest."

"Six," she said. "I've always wanted six."

His smile widened. "What a coincidence. That's how many I'd like, too."

"Seriously?"

"Seriously."

Tears flooded her eyes. "This is overwhelming."

"Oh, sweetheart, there's more."

"I don't know if I can handle more," she said with a shaky laugh.

It appeared, in this, he would give her no choice. Oliver rose, then dropped to his knee before her.

Shannon's breath hitched when he pulled out a velvet jeweler's box and flipped it open. The large diamond glittered in the sunlight. Smaller diamonds, but no less brilliant, surrounded the large marquis-cut stone.

"Shannon." He spoke her name softly, and in the quiet she heard the love, saw it reflected in his eyes.

"It's...it's the most beautiful ring I've ever seen."

His smile flashed and she knew her response had pleased him. He took her hand and focused those blue eyes directly on her as he began to speak.

"When I first saw you at the Superette, I was impressed by your kindness, your willingness to help a stranger find his way. Being around you, getting to know you, I realized just how special you are, and I began to fall in love." He squeezed her fingers. "If you count the days since we first met, we haven't known each other that long, but it feels as if I've known you forever. I've been waiting my whole life for you. Without a single doubt I know what we share is right and true and strong enough to last a lifetime."

It was quite a speech from a man not prone to verbosity. And she knew without a doubt the words came straight from his heart.

"Oh, Oliver." Joy sluiced through her veins. If this was a dream, Shannon prayed she'd never wake up.

"I promise no one will work harder to make you happy or cherish you more than me." His gaze searched hers. "And I will listen. Always. My life will never be complete without you beside me to share it. Will you marry me, Shannon? Will you be my wife and Ollie's mother?"

For several heartbeats, Shannon struggled to find her voice, to put into words all she was feeling.

"When I look into my heart, I see only you," she said finally. "I can't imagine growing old with anyone else. I love you so much. So yes, Oliver, I will marry you. And I'll be proud to be Ollie's mother."

Then the ring was on her finger. When he stood and pulled her into his arms, Shannon knew with absolute certainty there was no other place she wanted to be.

Not only for now, but for eternity.

Epilogue

The opulent hotel room on Buckingham Palace Road surrounded Shannon in a sweet cocoon of luxury. But the true treasure was the man sleeping beside her. She glanced at her husband, then at the large diamond solitaire on her left hand, now made complete by a wedding band.

Last week she and Oliver had tied the knot in Horseback Hollow, surrounded by family and friends. Two days ago, they'd flown to London, accompanied by her parents and brothers.

Oliver had insisted on paying for her family's trip to England and had gotten them all seats in first class. While in the UK, her parents and brothers were staying at his home in Knightsbridge. Shannon and Oliver would join them there at the end of the week.

She'd never thought she'd get her father on an airplane, much less out of the United States, but Shep had taken to England like a duck to water. Once he'd figured out how to use the Tube, her dad had been unstoppable. For her mother, this was the honeymoon she'd never had, but Oliver had waved aside her thanks, telling her that they were family now.

His family had embraced her just as easily. Last night, Brodie had hosted a reception for them, inviting not only family but Oliver's UK friends and business associates to celebrate their marriage at the swanky Savile Club in Mayfair.

The best part of the evening for Shannon was having the opportunity to get to know Brodie better. He wasn't as uptight as she first thought. She'd come away from their lengthy chat knowing she and Oliver's brother were destined to be good friends.

She was trying to decide whether to get up or go back to sleep when she felt Oliver stir.

"Can't you sleep?" he asked, pushing himself to a sitting position.

"Just admiring the view." She glanced around the sumptuous bridal suite in one of London's premier hotels. "This sure beats the B and B in Vicker's Corners."

"It's lovely here," he admitted. "I'm enjoying the view myself."

She turned to see what part of the room had captured his gaze. Was it the paintings? The mural on the ceiling? Or the opulent fixtures?

Instead she found his gaze focused directly on her.

Her skin heated beneath his gaze.

"The B and B was nice, too," he said, offering her a lazy smile. "I'll never forget that first night with my beautiful wife."

The images from their wedding day—and night—were forever etched in a special place in Shannon's heart. There were the vows they'd written and the scent from the orchids Oliver had had flown in because she'd mentioned once they were her favorite. Most of all, she'd never forget the look of love in his eyes when he'd seen her walking down the aisle on her father's arm.

"I like hearing you say 'my wife,'" she admitted. "Almost as much as I like saying 'my husband.'"

She snuggled beside him, her fingers toying with the hair on his chest. "Brodie mentioned last night he's taking full credit for us being together."

Oliver rolled his eyes and chuckled. "I don't know how he arrived at that conclusion, but it sounds like something my brother would say."

"Brodie is really very sweet." Shannon paused thoughtfully. "He's not nearly as stuffy as he first appears. I believe with a little help from the right woman…"

"You really think he just needs the right woman to warm him up?" Amusement ran through Oliver's voice like a pretty ribbon.

"I do."

"You know, I'm feeling a bit stuffy right now."

Shannon couldn't keep from smiling. "Is that code for you need some *warming up* yourself?"

"It is, indeed."

Oliver clasped her face gently in his hands, lowered his mouth to hers…then jerked back as the door to the bedroom was unceremoniously flung open.

Shannon gave a little yelp. "I thought we locked the door."

Oliver sat up straight, just in time to see his son race across the room, the nanny hot on his heels.

"Mama, Daddy," Ollie called out happily as he ran to his parents. "I come see you."

When he reached the bed, Ollie pulled himself up, then crawled over the covers, as quick and agile as a little monkey.

The drama continued when Barnaby appeared, zipping past the nanny, emitting deep woofs with each step. He reached the bedside and began to bark. Because of his short legs, the corgi required Shannon's help to make it to the top of the silk duvet.

"I'm so sorry, sir, ma'am. The little tyke got away from me." The distraught nanny's face was flushed and a strand of gray hair had come loose from her serviceable bun.

Though many relatives had offered to watch Ollie during their honeymoon, Shannon and Oliver had wanted the boy close, so they'd secured a suite and enlisted the help of Mrs. Crowder.

Ollie flung his arms around both parents, burrowing against them. He giggled as Barnaby reached him and began licking his face.

Nanny Crowder wrung her hands, obviously unsure if she should snatch her young charge and his pet out of his parents' honeymoon bed or simply beat a hasty retreat. "Oh, my. Oh, my. This will never do."

Oliver caught Shannon's eyes and they exchanged grins. It may have been a chaotic scene, at least to anyone unused to small boys and dogs, but this was his new reality.

He'd been blessed with a beautiful wife whom he adored, a son who brought joy to his life every day and a corgi that could always be counted on to liven things up.

"No worries, Mrs. Crowder," Oliver told the nanny, his heart overflowing with love and thankfulness. "This is all quite perfect."

* * * * *

*Don't miss the next installment of the new
Harlequin Special Edition continuity,*

THE FORTUNES OF TEXAS: COWBOY COUNTRY
*Matteo and his brother Cisco have always competed
over everything—until Matteo sets his eyes on Rachel
Robinson! But the girl of his dreams is clearly hiding
something—can their new love last in the face of
this bombshell?
Look for
MENDOZA'S SECRET FORTUNE
by*
USA TODAY *bestselling author Marie Ferrarella.
On sale March 2015, wherever
Harlequin books are sold.*

Matteo Mendoza is used to playing second fiddle to his brother Cisco…but not this time. Beautiful Rachel Robinson intrigues both siblings, but Matteo is determined to win her heart. Rachel can't resist the handsome pilot, but she's afraid her family secrets might haunt her chances at love. Can this Texan twosome find their very own happily-ever-after on the range?

Read on for a sneak preview of
MENDOZA'S SECRET FORTUNE by USA TODAY
bestselling author Marie Ferrarella, the third book in
THE FORTUNES OF TEXAS: COWBOY COUNTRY
continuity!

***

Matteo knew he should be leaving—and had most likely already overstayed—but he found himself wanting to linger just a few more seconds in her company.

"I just wanted to tell you one more time that I had a very nice time tonight," he told Rachel.

She surprised him—and herself when she came right down to it—by saying, "Show me."

Matteo looked at her, confusion in his eyes. Had he heard wrong? And what did she mean by that, anyway?

"What?"

"Show me," Rachel repeated.

"How?" he asked, not exactly sure he understood what she was getting at.

Her mouth curved, underscoring the amusement that was already evident in her eyes.

"Oh, I think you can figure it out, Mendoza," she told him. Then, since he appeared somewhat hesitant to put an actual meaning to her words, she sighed loudly, took hold of his button-down shirt and abruptly pulled him to her.

Matteo looked more than a little surprised at this display of proactive behavior on her part. She really was a firecracker, he thought.

The next moment, there was no room for looks of surprise or any other kind of expressions for that matter. It was hard to make out a person's features if their face was flush against another's, the way Rachel's was against his.

If the first kiss between them during the picnic was sweet, this kiss was nothing if not flaming hot. So much so that Matteo was almost certain that he was going to go up in smoke any second now.

The thing of it was he didn't care. As long as it happened while he was kissing Rachel, nothing else mattered.

***

Don't miss MENDOZA'S SECRET FORTUNE
by USA TODAY bestselling
author Marie Ferrarella,
the third book in
THE FORTUNES OF TEXAS: COWBOY COUNTRY
continuity!

Available March 2015, wherever
Harlequin® Special Edition books and ebooks are sold.